lady, drop dead

L A D Y

Lawrence Treat

DROP DEAD

London

ABELARD - SCHUMAN

New York

Toronto

LONDON   *Abelard Schuman Limited, 38 Russell Square*
NEW YORK   *Abelard Schuman Limited, 6 West 57 Street*
TORONTO   *Abelard Schuman Canada Limited, 81 John Street*
© Lawrence Treat 1960
Library of Congress Catalogue Card Number 60:7212

lady, drop dead

1

told him to take those papers, some building code junk, and

9

drop them off on the way home. Which Patrolman Mitch Taylor did, and then here he was in the Bierce Street neighbourhood and he got to thinking maybe he ought to go over to that address and give it a try. The thing was, he was a good cop and he had a nose for stuff like this, so he was pretty sure that something was going on and what was wrong with stopping in to have a look-see?

Mitch wasn't in uniform, of course. He was wearing the white, nylon shirt Amy had given him for his birthday, and it was a little short on shoulder-room. Not that he was a particularly big guy. He was medium height, maybe, but he was built solid, with plenty of chest.

His face, nicely padded against a sock in the jaw, literally or figuratively, and usually both, showed a guy who was pretty well satisfied to be himself. His dark brown eyes were clear as fresh oil, they seemed almost soft on account of those long lashes of his. His hair, thick and brushed back, was like wire.

He'd been an inspector on the Homicide Squad until a couple of months ago, and he still wasn't used to this patrolman stuff. In some ways, he didn't mind too much, he worked a regular shift and he could plan things with his family, he knew he'd be home on the dot, same time every afternoon. What burned him up, though, was that cut of five hundred cool, green pieces of lettuce. And why had it happened, huh? What for? All on account of a lousy ham sandwich.

If Mitch had been lucky, maybe Lieutenant Decker, in charge of Homicide, would have eaten that sandwich and got *his* guts twisted up. Maybe he'd have had those cramps and had to go around the corner just when this hold-up guy came down the back alley and walked out of the trap.

The thought of what the lieutenant would have done under the circumstances always made Mitch smile. But the smile never lasted, for Mitch was a realist. The facts were that the ham was contaminated and had done its work inside him, personally.

Mitch rarely thought of the interview he'd had with Bill

10

Decker. The lieutenant had said grimly, "Taylor, you've been on Homicide how long?"

"A little while," Mitch answered modestly.

"Two years. And, oh, brother!"

"I ate that sandwich without even leaving my post, and the doctor said it gave me ptomaine."

"What did you do to the doctor? Ask him the symptoms and then apply them?"

Mitch didn't answer. The funny thing was, he was kind of ashamed of the lieutenant for pouring it on like that. So Mitch sat up a little straighter, while Decker dumped himself forward and slapped his hand on the desk and started to make a speech.

"Maybe the Constitution gives you an inalienable right to tend to your personal needs, but I never saw worse timing. You're through."

So that was how it had all happened and why Mitch was back in uniform, in the Fourteenth Precinct. First off, it looked like a nice, quiet district and Mitch figured what the hell, at least they wouldn't work him too hard. Give him time to get acquainted, and he'd make out, the five hundred would start coming back to him. A little here, a little there. He wasn't greedy.

Then he began to learn the facts of life. The Fourteenth; they called it the gold coast on account of who lived here, but the gold was like the stuff in Fort Knox. You couldn't touch it. And the district was clean. No bars to shake down, no pool rooms to drop in on, no bookies to give you a cut, no nothing. You lived on your paycheck. Or, anyhow, the rest of the boys did.

Then one day, Mitch happened to notice this parking complaint. A car had blocked off part of a driveway on Bierce, and where were the police? It was crank stuff, you could see that right off, it was the kind of thing the sergeant said he'd look into, and then forgot about. But what stuck in Mitch's mind was that the car was a Cadillac and it was there because Vivian Vixen was giving some kind of a ball.

11

Mitch asked Oscar Henderson about her. Oscar was Mitch's partner, they rode around all day in a patrol car and upheld law and order, and Oscar knew the precinct like he was after their votes. But what it took him an hour to say was, Vivian Vixen had been a Hollywood star and then she had this accident and now she lived here like a female hermit, except she threw these parties and Oscar said there were all kinds of rumors about them.

So Mitch decided it was worth a try. If those shin-digs of hers were just that, she'd kiss him off. But if it turned out they weren't kosher, a morals charge or dope or something, maybe Mitch could work it up into a case that would land him right back on Homicide with that lousy pay-cut restored.

That was why Mitch was walking down the quiet residential block, looking for Number 1013. He found it on a sign by a high hedge. Behind was this white cottage, with small windows with heavy curtains across them.

He went up the path and rang the bell, and this radio voice jabbed at his ear. Then he saw the speaker built into the wall, at the right of the door, and he said who he was. Cop.

"I'd like to talk to you." he said in his high-pitched voice.

"You can talk from where you are."

Mitch didn't like that. First of all, how did he know who else was around? And in the second place, he wanted to see how Vivian Vixen fixed up her joint so he could come back and tell Amy about it. She was always picking up ideas that way, they had a kind of joke about it and he called himself her inferior decorator. So he didn't go for this business of talking through a machine.

"Lady," he said, "I don't do things that way."

"I'm quite alone," she said, "if that is your reason. But I happen to be dressing."

"Yeah, sure," he said. "Some other time, then. This'll wait."

A few seconds went by before she made up her mind. "The door is open, and you can step into the hall."

He turned the knob and went inside, and here he was in a short corridor with curtains over something at the end of it, and a table on one side with an orange-coloured vase on it. Some dames without too many clothes on were chasing some other dames around the vase. Greek, he guessed, and he took it in carefully so he could tell Amy about it.

The door on the left was ajar, and Vivian Vixen spoke from behind it. "Well?" she said, and her voice smoked like dry ice.

"It's about those parties of yours," Mitch said, sort of feeling his way along. "We had a couple of complaints, I thought you ought to know about them so we can head them off."

"*We!*" she said. Even through the door, she could pack an awful lot into just one word. But that was what made her an actress.

Mitch went on cheerfully. "Protecting people, that's my job. I figure if I can stop trouble before it starts, I'm doing my work, and I make it easier for the both of us."

"What trouble?" she demanded.

"You know the answer, better than me."

"By what right," she began angrily. But Mitch cut her off fast.

"No right. I'm just trying to do you a favour, that's all."

"I think," she said, and the contempt in her voice felt like she was clawing at him with her nails, "I think I know what you mean by doing a favor. What is your name?"

Mitch didn't care for the question. It sounded like she was going to twist this little talk around and complain to the lieutenant, and then Mitch would be on the carpet, but good. Still, he'd gone this far and he wasn't going to back out. And, anyhow, she could find out who he was, that would be easy. So he answered the question straight. "Taylor," he said.

She began laughing. "How much are you trying to shake me down for?" she demanded. "Will a hundred do?"

For a second or so, Mitch thought she was kidding, and then he wished she was. Because this was dirty money, you could smell it a mile off. He was used to kind of hanging onto the last car of the gravy train, that was all right. When the rest of the boys were collecting, he usually got his, on account of he had a wife and family to support, and who was he to

13

buck the system? Clean money, everybody took it and so did he. But a hundred was an out-and-out bribe, you didn't hand out that sort of dough unless you were buying a lot more than Mitch was willing to sell.

So he didn't know what to do. He stood there and muttered, "Yeah—well—you see—" He wished he'd never come here, he wanted out but he didn't know how to swing it without he'd feel like a prize jackass.

That was when he heard a car outside. With the front door wide open, he could just about see through the hedge, and here was a pretty good chance to blow. So he said, "Looks like you got company. I'll step outside and see, huh?"

So he went out and closed the door, and then here was this big, dark-haired, good-looking boy walking up with a grin on his face and acting like the rooster that owned the joint.

He said to Mitch, "Excuse me," and then he stuck his map up against the speaker and said, "Viv? It's me. And there's somebody waiting."

"I know. He claims he's a police officer. Would you ask him for his identification, and then come in?"

"Sure thing."

Mitch showed the guy his potsy, and watched him walk in and leave Mitch on the doorstep like some jerk that couldn't even speak the language. Then after a while the door opened and the guy came out with a roll of bills and handed them to Mitch.

"She said this was for you."

Mitch looked at the money without taking it. "What's that for?"

"Pay-off, she says."

Mitch grunted, and he was offended, besides. Even if he'd expected to take the dough, did she think he was dumb enough to take it in front of a witness? There were ways of doing things, but this one was all wrong.

"You're nuts," he said coldly. "I ought to bring you in for trying to bribe an officer."

"I'm doing what she told me to, so lay off, will you?"

14

"Give it back, and tell her I don't know what the hell she's talking about."

The dark guy shrugged. "Okay," he said. "Whatever you say." And he slipped inside.

For the next few hours, Mitch felt virtuous, but then the feeling wore off and he began wondering. Maybe Vivian Vixen had so much lettuce that she threw it away. And what was wrong with taking dough when you didn't know what it was for? He felt like a dope, he told himself he ought to go back and find out what the score was. In a few days, he promised himself. But he'd give it a rest, why push it? He'd wait until he was in the neighborhood again.

But the worst of it was, it hit him that maybe this dark-haired guy had kept the hundred for himself. Suppose Mitch had just handed it out for free, then what? How could a guy respect himself, after that?

2

EVEN THE BEST of them can't tail a man day after day without being noticed, and Hank Greenleaf was far from the best. And besides, he stood out like a hussar.

He was a big guy with dark, flashing eyes and jet-black hair combed back in a reckless sweep. He looked as if his teeth could crunch iron, and his laugh made you think he had the world by the pig-tail and loved tossing it around.

His appearance, however, was deceptive, for Hank was a worrier and he hated his work. Bad hours, irregular income, eternities of waiting. Setting up his own investigation agency had been a mistake, and the sooner he wound it up, the better.

Take this Drury business, for instance. A wealthy and respected citizen was having an affair with a world-famous

15

actress. The set-up reeked with glamor and fumed with mystery. If the things that went on behind the heavy drawn curtains of her house ever came out, they'd feed the prurient and fill the tabloids for six months. Writers would make thousands out of it and publishers would make millions, but Hank would merely be advised to buy orthopedic shoes. Fallen arches, the doctor would tell him. Too much standing around.

The only thing that kept Hank going was the hope of a job as probation officer, after the exam came up in the fall. It would mean a civil-service rating and a paycheck every month. That was for him, and he always kept the Manual for Probation Officers with him, together with a standard text on penology or some related subject.

He didn't have the college credits, but his experience gave him an edge and, under the law, if he passed high enough he could get the appointment and make up the credits later on. And even if he didn't, he'd merely be reclassified and reassigned, probably as an investigator. But once he was in civil-service, he was sure of a job.

He lived for the day when he'd receive a notice that he'd qualified, for he had to know where he stood. He liked answers better than questions, facts better than theories and habits better than novelty. Which was why the Drury case bothered him out of all proportion, like an itch without a reason for it.

The case started out normally enough. A wealthy clubwoman named Mrs. Drury hired him to follow her husband, and within a week Hank's reports supported her suspicions the way rocks support Manhattan. At which point Hank's job should have been finished, save for a possible court appearance to give testimony. At his usual fee.

But Mrs. Drury was no ordinary woman. She seemed to hunger for constant proof of her husband's transgressions, and Hank got the idea that a let-up would disappoint her.

Maybe she just needed the excitement, for she was certainly endowed with a constitution capable of absorbing shocks. In her late forties, she was big, energetic and forceful, with a duffle-bag of a bosom leading the way wherever she went. With her clean, straight features and dark, seething eyes, she must have been beautiful once; now, she was regal.

She had a way of bossing Hank around as if she'd hired him to play doormat. Which was all right with him. He kept vigil and cashed the pretty, pink checks that she sent him regularly. They enabled him to rent a summer bungalow at Lake Pride and install his old man and his kid in it. With Jean spending her vacation up there, too, taking care of them.

Then one day little Drury went and threw a monkey-wrench into the hitherto orderly procedure of sin. He pulled his Cadillac over to the curb, stepped out and trotted back to where Hank was parked.

"Excuse me," the little man said humbly, "but you're Mr. Greenleaf, aren't you? The investigator that Mrs. Drury hired?"

Hank gazed at the cherubic face, uncrowned with hair. Drury's fingers brushed the door of Hank's car timidly, then withdrew as if he was afraid Hank might object.

"What gives you that idea?" Hank asked.

"I found your reports in her bureau drawer. And I know you've been following me, I see you all the time. I feel I know you, as if we were friends."

If Hank had had any pride in his work, he might have put up an argument. Or at least pounded down on Drury and told him to get the hell out and mind his own business. But Hank didn't give a damn.

"So?" he said vaguely.

"I'd like to ask you a favor," Drury said, and his whole soul seemed to float up into his solemn, gray eyes.

"Yes? What?"

"I wish you wouldn't follow so closely. She—" Drury never mentioned her by name. He referred to his wife as Mrs. Drury, but *she* was always she. "She doesn't like it."

"Nobody does," Hank observed.

"Oh, I do, it makes me feel important." Drury smiled lamely, as if apologizing for his frisky ego which hadn't quite grown up. "But she's different, and it annoys her. I don't have to tell you why."

"I'll try to be unobtrusive," Hank remarked.

Drury's eyes lit up at the big word, as if he'd discovered a fellow egghead. "What I hoped," he said meekly, "was that I could tell you where we were going, and then you could meet us and check up. I'll pay you extra for keeping out of sight."

"Unethical," Hank said. "Taking money from both sides—I could lose my license. Besides, the whole idea is wrong. You're not supposed to fraternize with me. I'm the enemy."

"I'm no good at disliking people. Mr. Greenleaf, you can trust me." Drury's gray eyes had that pleading look again. "Tonight, for instance, I'm on my way to her house, and then we're going to Gino's for dinner. We have a reservation for eight-thirty."

Gino's, where you ate by candlelight at twenty dollars a person, minimum, and the wine-list started at ten bucks a bottle.

"You usually have dinner at her house," Hank said. "Why the change?"

"Celia, her cook, is in the country, and this seemed the time for her to start going out in public and try leading a normal life again."

"Just the two of you having dinner?"

"Of course. A third person would make her self-conscious."

"I see," Hank said thoughtfully.

He glowered at Drury. The little man's proposition, despite his naïve manner, sounded like a trick to shake Hank off. And yet, all Drury had to do was tell his wife he knew she'd hired an investigator and had seen the reports, and then she'd fire Hank. No more pink checks.

So why not go along with the guy?

Hank nodded, took out a piece of paper and scribbled some notes. "Gino's—that's on South Paine, isn't it? Gino's at eight-thirty. I'll watch for you."

Drury held out his small hand. "Thanks, Mr. Greenleaf. I'll tell her, she'll be relieved."

18

Hank watched the Cadillac drive off in the direction of Vivian Vixen's house. As soon as the car was out of sight, he headed for a phone-booth and called Gino's. By pretending he was from Drury's office and had an important message, Hank extracted the information that Drury did have an eight-thirty reservation. Apparently, the little guy was playing it straight.

During the weeks that followed, Ronald Drury formed the habit of confiding his plans for the evening, and he and Hank built up a pleasant, although unorthodox friendship. Drury supplied details that Hank incorporated in his reports, and unquestionably Mrs. Drury was getting her money's worth. Hank was lulled into a sense of security and it seemed to him that the present arrangement could carry him right up to his civil-service job. He had ample time to read and study, the money poured in, and he was reasonably content. Until the afternoon Mrs. Drury stormed into the cubicle that Hank called an office.

"Mr. Greenleaf," she said in a voice that blared through the entire loft, "your reports are boring."

"Sorry," he said, pushing the probation manual to the side of his desk. "I didn't realize you were out for amusement."

"Please don't be facetious," she said sharply. "You write as if you were composing a railroad time-table, but I hardly came here to criticize your literary style." She lowered her voice, and her large, handsome features twitched with embarrassment. "I want more facts. Not just where they go and how long they stay, but what they really do."

"If I understand correctly," Hank said, "why don't I just set up a raid and catch them in the act, and then you'll have your divorce evidence and that will be the end of it?"

"I don't want a divorce," she said angrily. "Do you think I'd let him leave me? He's my husband. And for your edification, we're both grandparents."

"Then what do you want?" Hank asked.

"I'd like to know the details of what they say and how they behave together. Their very words, as if I were there."

"Kind of an impossibility, isn't it?"

"I believe there are such things as recording devices. Isn't *bugging* the term you'd use?"

Hank ran his hand through his black, glossy hair and wished he looked more like a peanut and less like a conqueror. "Can't do it," he said. "Illegal. And my advice is, stay away from anybody who'd do it. You'd be asking for trouble."

"Then go see her and get the information directly. Extracting information is your business, isn't it?"

"Sure, but what do want me to find out? What are you after?"

The duffle-bag across Edith Drury's chest heaved. "It's quite simple. My husband is having an affair, and it isn't right. I propose to stop it."

"How? You have evidence. How is more of the same going to help?"

"That," she said haughtily, "is none of your concern."

"Sure. But Mrs. Drury, how can I operate when I don't know where I'm going? What's your objective? Because unless I know it, I'm helpless."

"What I'm after," she said icily, "is the means of breaking up this *liaison*, so that he'll be sorry for what he's done."

"I still don't see where I come in."

Mrs. Drury licked her full, red lips. "Marriage is a complicated thing. Ronald has been my husband for twenty-five years. He's made quite a good thing for himself with my money, and in fairness to him I'll admit that he's increased it substantially, but it's still my money and he has no right to spend it on her."

Hank gave up. "Sure," he said wearily. "I'll keep working."

She raised her head and said in a clear, challenging voice, "You don't understand. I've suffered. People are talking behind my back. They feel sorry for me and they say, 'Poor Mrs. Drury, how can she stand it?' Well, I can stand it nicely, but I won't permit people to pity me. Or laugh at me, either."

For a moment, Hank felt sorry for her. The way she kept licking her lips, the unconscious movement of her fingers that scraped at the desk and rubbed at the pages of the manual, turned up a corner and then pressed it down—she was nervous, embarrassed, ill at ease. Nevertheless he kept probing, like a doctor lancing a wound without regard for the immediate hurt.

"Let's see if we can really spell this out," he said, "and then we'll drop it. What Miss Vixen thinks of you and what Mr. Drury has told her about you—is that it?"

Edith Drury exploded. "No," she said. "How can you be so dense? Mr. Greenleaf, are you married?"

"I was."

"Then perhaps you realize how emotional a woman is, and what a terrible thing it is when her husband no longer cares." She squeezed the manual and then released it and lowered her hand to her lap. "It's not an easy thing to tell a stranger," she continued shakily, "and you force me to admit things I'd rather not say."

"Just tell me what to ask Vivian," he said obstinately.

"That's up to you, but she's a vile, grasping creature, without conscience. I want Ron to see her as she is, so that he'll hate her and regret what he's done." She worked at her lips again. "I'm a little upset. Would you mind getting me a glass of water?"

"Sure," Hank said. "Glad to."

He got up and went out to the water-cooler.

The picture began to come clear, finally. She wanted to cheapen and degrade Vivian Vixen and destroy her for Ron. Then Edith Drury could make him squirm. She could put him back on his leash and parade him around, so that the world could see she'd won.

It wasn't a nice picture and Hank didn't care to be party to it, until he remembered that Ron had married her for her money. The mistake had been made twenty-five years ago, and Hank wasn't interested in playing God. He was merely trying to make a living.

When he returned to his office, Edith Drury was staring thoughtfully at the portable typewriter in its carrying-case.

She had made up her lips again and she was calm, her hand steady. As she took the paper cup and sipped, her fingers left a red smudge halfway up.

"Do you do your own typing?" she asked.

He supposed he should have said no, he was too busy, he always dictated. Then he could have added that he'd given his secretary the afternoon off. Sure. Put up a front, impress the clients.

He said, "Yes."

"I thought so. You make so many typographical errors."

"Thanks," he said drily.

"I don't usually give confidences, and particularly to people I scarcely know. And you didn't make it easy for me, either."

"I'm trying to do a job."

"Naturally," she said, nodding. "And I pay you to follow my orders, and I pay you quite well."

Hank grinned. "Our business relations have been pretty satisfactory."

"Then just remember that my motives are distinctly not your business. You'll see this person, then?"

"Right. And I can tell you now—my report is going to be dull."

"I don't see how it can be."

"You forget my literary style," Hank said. "I guess I'm just a dull person, and everybody else seems the same. Nice and ordinary. No excitement, no glamor, no trappings. But you'll get the facts."

Edith Drury stood up, put on her gloves and picked up her purse. "I want them soon," she said. "I can be extremely impatient."

The next day he went to see Vivian Vixen.

He knew a good deal about her, as did other people who kept their ears open. Twenty years ago—Hank had been eleven, and uninterested in civil-service jobs—she'd been one of Hollywood's greats, turning out a couple of pictures a year. Whatever she did was sure-fire at the box-office. She was beautiful, she was glamorous, and she could act. Her face, sensitive and mobile, gave depth and imagination to every role she created. She had a golden touch at her fingertips, and a golden body to back it up.

Then came the automobile accident, and after that, nothing. The name of Vivian Vixen was no longer in the news, or even in the gossip columns. Rumors were rife. She'd lost both legs, she was blind, her face had been horribly scarred. Nobody knew, nobody was certain, even, that she was alive, until she came back here, to her home town.

There was no reception and there were no interviews. The papers maintained a discreet silence. But here and there, information begain to trickle in. She'd bought a house, she was remodeling it. She'd sold the house, moved into another. The buyers of the one she'd left found evidence of a strange cult. The cellar had contained an altar, the living-room bore marks of curious installations. The carpenters who had worked on them knew nothing, they hadn't seen the result. They'd built platforms and wooden archways, and that was that.

To be sure, there were gatherings at her house, but the people who attended them said little, and differed materially on the meaning of the mystic rites in which they'd taken part. On one point, however, there was complete agreement. Nobody saw her. She stayed behind a screen. She was a disembodied voice, the high priestess and the exalted presence on which no eye could look.

Hank spent an evening watching her guests come and go to one of those séances. He counted seventeen people, of whom all but two were men. They looked like business executives, and they arrived in expensive cars. They stayed about two hours.

Hank noticed a catering truck parked in the driveway of her house, and the next day he located one of the crew and picked up a conversation.

"That's the third time I worked one of her parties," the guy said, "and it's always the same thing. Buffet in the library, with plenty of champagne, and strict orders for us to stay out

23

of the next room. And there's this cook of hers, a big black mammy, bossing us around."

"What do they talk about, when they come in to eat? You hear plenty, don't you?"

"They talk about her and they wonder what she looks like. But they don't know, they don't get to first base on it."

"But what's it all about? What do they come for?"

"She shows off her movies," said the caterer, and grimaced.

In the course of following Drury, Hank had seen her often, but always at a distance. He noticed that her hats were designed for concealment, and she was careful never to let anyone approach her. According to rumor, she wore a mask, a replica of her face in the days when she'd made one of her greatest pictures. *The Odalisque*, the harem girl.

Several times, however, Hank had examined her through field-glasses, and he had glimpsed a face that was alabaster white and completely expressionless. The lips could talk, the eyes could turn, but they moved as from a death-mask, fixed and inanimate. A plastic surgon had restored her features, but the muscles and nerves were non-existent.

Hank called on her without making an appointment. She lived in one of the older and wealthier sections of the city, and he drove down a wide pleasant street divided by a center row of maples. It ended in a broad circle where a half-dozen cars were clustered, as if the neighborhood used the area for community parking.

Hank got out. Vivian's house, the last one on the street, was hidden from view by a high, privet hedge. He went through the narrow gap and saw a Cape Cod cottage, with a pair of wooden benches set in the gabled entrance. The metal door-mat was bent, and it creaked under his feet. When he rang the bell, a voice answered through a grating that screened a speaker.

"Who is there?" The voice was arresting, it was a singer's voice that vibrated with a complex of disturbing overtones.

"You don't know me," Hank said. "The name's Greenleaf."

"Oh, the detective."

24

"Not exactly. But Mr. Drury—"

"I know who you are, Ron told me. What do you want?"

"I'd like to explain a few things, and I think you'll be interested."

There was a long silence before the voice said: "The door's open. Come in, and please wait in the hall."

Even outside, standing in bright sunlight and hearing her throaty voice filtered through the speaker, Hank had been aware of a magnetism. But here in the hallway and with the door behind him, he felt the close presence of her unsettling personality: it was in the yellowed light that came from concealed bulbs and fell softly, like mist. It bathed the polish of the woodwork and was lapped up by the dark, fuzzy wallpaper. But it exploded sharply in the altarpiece at the end of the corridor.

There, framed by a pair of draped curtains, was the figure of a madonna in blue. Angels floated past her and reached out, as if seeking the favor of touching her robe.

Slowly, Hank's eyes lifted to her face. He frowned, licked his lips. This was the Vivian Vixen of twenty years ago, radiantly passionate, the lips soft, wet, trembling, and the face shimmering with some deep, inner glory. The paradox of that veiled, madonna-like spirituality combined with the open invitation of the sensual mouth, shook you. The complexities of her character were obvious, but you didn't know which facet you'd meet. The result was to put you on the defensive, so that you met her on her terms, not yours.

Hank stood there, gazing fixedly. He coughed. If Vivian was anything like her picture, he had some facts for Mrs. Drury, and she wouldn't like them. Except that the Vivian in front of him, if she still existed, operated behind concealed layers of intricateness, like the tubes and condensers of a TV set that took something out of the air and slapped the result in front of your eyes.

Hank stepped back. He turned, frowning, and stared at the dark heavy drapes over a doorway. The low contralto voice spoke from behind it.

"Come in, Mr. Greenleaf." He parted the curtains.

In the semi-light, he saw that one side of the room was plastered with photographs of moviedom's top stars. The remaining walls were covered with fluted drapes, gray-brown. Against a white, oval insert, he noticed a richly-jeweled dagger in the shape of a cross. He walked past it, and she was there, waiting.

The couch on which she lay was on a raised dais and was framed like an old-fashioned closet-bed, with a low overhang. The mattress was covered with a large, tawny lion skin. She was wearing a white gown, pleated and flowing in endless folds, and tight only at the green belt which clasped her waist. The light poured down on her body, but her face, barely visible, was in heavy shadow.

"Henry Greenleaf," she said, as if she were chanting a prayer, "you have come here to learn, and you will learn, but not what you expect."

"What do I expect?" he asked, bowled over by her speech, anxious to hold off for a few moments until he could adjust to her and pick his best approach.

She extended her arm, slender and firm as a girl's, with the wrist bent and the fingers pointing to a chair set in the full glare of a spotlight.

It was quite an act. Her voice, rare as the tones of a Stradivarius, created an atmosphere and a mood. The setting was good theater, and the technician in her had created it artfully. Seated, Hank could look straight out at the supple body in the silken, Grecian gown, but if he turned his eyes toward her face, he was blinded.

He tried to move the chair. It was screwed down tight.

"I permit no one to look at me," she said, "until I have seen into their hearts and measured their compassion. I have been made to suffer, but my suffering is shared only by the chosen few."

"How do you choose them?"

"*They* choose *me*. Mr. Greenleaf—Henry." Her hand moved along her thigh, rested with the tapering fingers outspread.

"Both your names are so awkward. I shall have to give you another."

"Most people call me Hank. I'm not a formal guy."

"Hank." She repeated it slowly. "Ah, Hank. Have you ever heard of the literature of Zen?"

"Vaguely," he said, floundering beyond his depth and wondering whether to float along with the tide or to fight. "Zen Buddhism, or something."

"Ronald and I talk of it a great deal, and in our humble way we try to live it. He has taught me."

"Anything he did," Hank said, "would be done humbly. And with gentleness."

"I love him," she said, "like a brother. I sense him, I feel him."

Hank made no comment. She had to go through with her performance, and by and by she'd get tired of it. He hoped.

"I feel you, too. Hank, you have suffered deeply."

Again he made no comment. He supposed she knew. He had in fact, mentioned something of it to Ron.

"I feel the currents," she said, using the not inconsiderable talents of her voice. "They are tragic."

"You're getting close," Hank said, "but not close enough. Give me a detail or two."

"*You* tell *me*."

It was the second time she'd used the same trick of emphasis. *They* choose *me*. *You* tell *me*. The same intonation, the same implication, the same switch of thought. It struck him that he was here to find out something for a client, and that there were a lot of ways of doing it. It he had to pretend, make like a sucker, go along with her act, what did he have to lose? He could play tag her way, it would set up a friendly, personal atmosphere. Next time, or the time after, he'd reverse the field and ask her a few questions.

"Tell me about yourself," she said.

He gazed at her. The golden body, the face that was blotted out. Phony or not, she was human, she'd been hurt, and she'd

27

had the courage to set up a new life. She was trying. And after all the Hollywood razzle-dazzle, it wasn't easy.

Tell me about yourself. Who didn't want to dish out his autobiography, when there was somebody to listen? And besides, she had a presence, a personality that carried you along.

"Cars," he said. "I always loved cars. When I was a kid, I worked at a gas-station, and then later on I worked in a parking lot, and after a while I got a job with an automobile finance company, repossessing cars. I was good at it, too. And I went to night school, regularly."

"Yes," she said. "I know. I know all about you."

She didn't, of course. The phoniness pushed through, like an uplift bra taking all the credit when there was a perfectly good, warm breast behind it.

He spoke to the breast, and figuratively he laid his head on it. He found it soft and warm and receptive.

"I don't usually talk about these things," he said. "Most people find them boring, and I can stand on my own two feet. But—you asked for it."

"I am the all-spirit," she said, intoning her words impressively. "I am the earth and the water, the womb and the grave."

"I'd rather talk to a person. Maybe Ron likes poetry and high-sounding rhetoric, but it usually leaves me cold."

"I am truth, I am love. You're not speaking to me, because I am disembodied. You are communing with yourself and examining your soul. I merely happen to be here." She raised her hand, with the palm extended outward, and she seemed to be pleading. Her voice dropped and it vibrated with urgency and warmth. "Please tell me," she said.

He started out haltingly, but he found that it did him good to talk. He told her how he'd married a slim, willowy blond with a zest for life, TV style. Sherry wanted fun with breakfast and seven Sundays a week, she wanted a flashy car, expensive clothes and bottles of perfume strewn at her feet. It became increasingly evident to Hank that he and wife lacked a meeting of the minds.

28

He worried about the years ahead, but he had too much loyalty and too much devotion to make an end of what had been launched with so bright a beginning. Nevertheless the tarnish grew and the gleam faded.

"She was the wrong person for me," he said. "She started playing around with a fast crowd, and we had arguments. I used to lie next to her and wish she was dead, so that I could construct a life of grace and dignity, instead of trying to act out a bunch of commercials. Later on, death-wishes kick back, they haunt you, especially when—"

The arrival of a son and heir gave the future a different shape, and he had hopes that Sherry would accept the responsibilities of motherhood. All he asked for was a reasonably peaceful coexistence. Then one night she and some friends went skyrocketing down a highway with irresistible force. Hank was left a widower with a small, human bundle named Toby, and a twitch in his stomach every time he saw a car exceeding the speed limit.

He found he could no longer work with cars, but his reputation and previous accomplishments put his talents in demand, and he capitalized on them by opening his own investigation agency. Tracing cars, tracing people—he decided the techniques were similar. But after a success or two, he settled down to the humdrum disillusionment of the divorce trade.

What concerned him most, however, was trying to be a halfway decent father. And that involved, as a corollary, the acquisition of a halfway decent mother.

Greenleaf, senior, was a retired grounds-keeper at the ball park. Being aware of Hank's problem and having Hank's welfare at heart, he invited Jean Fergus into the house for the summer.

She was a distant cousin. She taught school, she understood children, and she made it plain that she was available. Being maternal, she attempted to regularize Hank's life. She taught him to turn out lights in order to save electricity, to wash his hands before meals, and to balance a checkbook regularly.

29

Her attainments and common sense were prodigious. In addition she was gifted with a normal human body, not yet put to its proper use, but prepared to be. She could smile pleasingly, read small print and sew on buttons.

She had decided that Hank ought to be a cop and she kept telling him about a friend of hers, Amy Taylor, who was married to a patrolman. As Jean expanded on the idyllic life of the Taylors, Hank came to resent the very name. These holier-than-thou guys annoyed him, and he hoped he'd never have to meet this Taylor. Still, Hank had to admit that Jean would make him a good wife. Nothing like Sherry.

Sitting there in the nailed-down chair, in the glare of the spotlight, he glossed over the role of Jean and gave a thumb-nail sketch of himself.

"Most of the time I'm a pretty ordinary guy," he said, "but I go off the handle every once in a while. I've got a streak in me that likes to take a chance. Although I usually regret it, later on."

"We are all of us two people," she said. "Our two sides wage perpetual war."

"Sure," he said. "So when I opened my agency. I had an idea I might run into something a little off-beat. Something interesting, like a murder. But I didn't, and now I don't care."

"You care," she said. "It will happen. You will soar to heights and descend into valleys that you never dreamed existed."

That was too much for him, and he stood up. "Skip it," he said. "You're just throwing words at me and trying to make an impression."

"I've made my impression," she said. "I like you." Her voice seemed to falter for a moment. Then her guard was up, she was the high priestess again, intoning, seeking to control.

"Come back," she said, "and all shall be revealed. Through the gateway of the body."

"If you mean what I think you do," he began. But she interrupted.

"All," she said. "All that is sacred and beautiful. All that the gods permit shall be yours to feed on. You will know when. And now—go."

He stood up, and abruptly she switched out the light and plunged the room in semi-darkness. There was only the light in the hall to show him the way out. He headed for it.

"Miss Vixen," he said. "You're a prize screwball."

"Sure," she said, in a normal voice. "And so are you."

3

IT WAS HOT THAT SUNDAY, otherwise Hank would never have done it. But the thermometer was in the nineties and the heavy, stifling air hung motionless over the city. Mascara melted and lipstick oozed. Women dressed with revealing immodesty, and nobody wanted them. Too hot. The sun cooked pavements and parched lawns and boiled up automobile engines.

And that, too, was why he did it. His ancient car couldn't have kept up the pace. The radiator would have steamed over and he'd have been left miles behind. And, finally, he trusted Drury.

At eleven A.M., Hank parked across the street from the Kendrick Arms, where Drury lived in expensive unhappiness. Hank took out his worn manual with the ripped binding and opened it to the section on the state probation laws. But, with one eye on the doorway of the apartment, he found it difficult to concentrate.

Besides, he kept thinking of Vivian. Fame, glory beyond dreams, and then all of it yanked away. She must have been in a hell of a state when she moved here, and from the act she'd put on for Hank, he could guess what her parties must have been like, in the pre-Drury days. The pagan goddess intoning her abracadabra to a spell-bound audience.

She needed those audiences, too. She couldn't face people on a normal basis, so she fixed up her reclining thrones and wooden altars, and played her role to the hilt. And from what Hank had heard, at the end of the evening the masked goddess picked her mortal lover and turned out the lights. And probably kicked him out before dawn, too.

Then Drury had come into her life. A mild little guy with a bossy wife, he'd broken down the barriers and offered his gentle, undemanding friendship. To which Vivian had reacted. She was trying to find a new way of life in which the things she'd lost didn't count.

The Zen business was Drury's contribution. Hank didn't know whether Vivian understood any of it, or whether some quality in Drury soothed her and appealed to her, quite apart from his precepts. For Drury was a philosopher by nature, and he lived quietly and was much alone. Although he'd married a few million and had increased his fortune through shrewd, real-estate operations, he didn't throw his money around. He ate well and he drove a Cadillac, but otherwise his wealth was rarely in evidence.

Hank had trailed Vivian and Drury often enough to see her dependence on him and to catch their simple, unconscious gestures of affection. They liked being together. They went to the movies, they drove around the city or out to the country, and occasionally they weekended at a big, chateau-like house near Raffneyville, some fifty-odd miles from the city.

Hank made enquiries about the place. It was owned by Richard Marlin, the real-estate operator. He'd sold Vivian both the houses she'd lived in, and she had had extensive business dealings with him. Apparently Marlin had acquired the estate for resale, and couldn't find a customer. Meanwhile, he let his office staff use it weekends, he brought out clients whom he wished to impress, and he permitted Vivian to install herself in the privacy of one wing.

In the course of his investigation, Hank had visited the mansion at Raffneyville. Pretending he was lost, he'd gone to

32

the kitchen door and made friends with Celia, the cook. Like some black snowman, she was constructed of large spheres overlaid with shiny lacquer. She was too top-heavy to lift her feet more than an inch or two above the ground, and she rocked along cautiously, like a tugboat hitting a ground swell. She was equally broad, but inside, she was all heart, and her round, beaming face was too small to hold in her smiling. It spilled out into her voice and her gestures, and it seemed to season the hot cornbread, soaked in syrup and served with bacon, with which she filled Hank's grateful stomach.

She'd been easy to question, for a show of kindliness opened up floodgates of talk. She explained that in the fall and winter she came to Miss Vivian's every afternoon and stayed until after dinner. Miss Vivian couldn't get along without her. But Lord love you, Celia exclaimed—with a chance to come out here and live in a castle instead of being cooped up in a city slum, could she turn down Paradise?

Celia admitted that being without a cook was hard on Miss Vivian, but Celia had rights, too. And Miss Vivian was up here for half the summer and she had a maid in town to wash up, and only a saint would have stayed in town.

But Celia was no saint. She made that plain. Miss Vivian was a lot closer to sainthood. She missed out by the margin of a few transgressions, but the time would come when she'd turn her back on sinning. And the best of saints made their way up, through error and vice, and she, Celia, didn't give two hoots for them as was born saints and had always been that way. Sin first and then repent, was what Celia believed, and the day would come for Miss Vivian.

Hank finished the cornbread and brought Celia back to a recital of facts. According to Celia, Miss Vivian, the poor lamb, loved it up here. She mingled freely with the Marlin group, but whenever there were guests she spent her days in seclusion with Drury and emerged only in the evening, to sit in a corner of the unlit porch and hold court. Had Hank ever seen her? Lord love him—some day he might get to

33

C

know her. And would he like some more of that cornbread? She never did see anybody admire it so much.

Hank smiled at the recollection. Celia was quite a dame, he reflected. And so was Vivian, and he wondered how she was getting along in the city heat. Then his eye, precise as a camera, registered a figure leaving the front door of the Kendrick Arms. His client, Edith Drury. Eleven-forty-five.

He watched her wheel, head for the boulevard. She held her head high and marched briskly, as if she was determined to overcome the weather. She kept up her pace until she reached the bus stop at the corner. There, she retreated into the shade, opened her bag and mopped her face.

Hank wondered why she took the bus when she had her own car. Maybe she liked buses. Or maybe she was trying to save money, after learning that Drury had presented his girl friend with three thousand dollars.

Drury had mentioned the gift last Monday, while talking to Hank on the street. "You want Mrs. Drury to know about it?" Hank had asked in surprise.

"Certainly. She's entitled to all the information she can get."

A curious little guy. But he was engaged in marital warfare with a superior force, and he had to use guerrilla tactics.

Hank watched the superior force step to the curb and hail a bus as if she was semaphoring signals to a torpedo boat. She boarded the platform with a strong, springy push of her legs. Gears ground, a superheated motor roared, and the bus plowed off.

Hank unbuttoned the top of his blue sport-shirt and fanned his skin. The heavy, humid air absorbed no moisture, and he let the shirt sag against his chest, where it stuck. His neck oozed perspiration that slid slowly down his sternum.

He gave up fighting the heat, and he thought of one of the times he'd followed Drury and Vivian on a picnic. Through a pair of fieldglasses he'd watched them stroll hand in hand across a meadow until they found a quiet spot protected by the rolling ground. There, they made themselves

34

comfortable on the grass and opened their lunch basket. Afterward, Drury stretched out with his head in her lap, while she read to him. Occasionally she put the book aside, and they talked.

A nice, intimate, bucolic scene. Hank's account, however, was laconic: "Subject and VV drove to the country, had picnic lunch, returned to VV's house at 5.10. Dinner, with champagne. Private showing of one of her films, no other guests. Subject left at 12.20 A.M."

Drury had supplied the touches about the champagne and the movie.

Well, what else could Hank learn about the pair of them? He thought of the report he'd eventually send to Mrs. Drury. "VV interested in mysticism, has need of privacy, and is fond of Mr. D." That's what it would come down to, and Hank was damned if he'd supply details. He was an investigator, and not a psychoanalyst.

He began worrying about that report, and then, at 12.05, precisely, Drury's Cadillac nosed up the ramp of the apartment house garage. Drury waved and parked further down the street. Hank, wiping the sweat from his forehead, got out. When Drury swung a door open, Hank stepped into the cool, pleasant interior.

"Your air-conditioning works," he said, sinking into the cushion of the front seat.

Drury nodded. "I'm sorry you had to wait there, in the heat."

"Got to earn my pay."

"You have too much conscience," Drury said, smiling. "You could have picked up a phone and asked me where I was going, and when."

"Well, where? And when?"

"To Raffneyville, after lunch. Marlin's trying to sell her the property out there and she put down a three-thousand-dollar deposit. That's the money I just gave her, and I'm going to make him return it."

"A tall order."

35

"No, it ought to be easy, because Dick Marlin needs her. She's been buying houses from him, living in them for a while and then putting them up for sale. People love to own a house she's lived in, it increases the value. So, if he wants to continue the arrangement, he can't afford to make her angry."

"You seem to know all the angles."

"I ought to know real estate by now, I've been at it long enough." Drury's lips firmed up and he spoke with the crisp authority of a business man. "Marlin's over-invested, he has too many syndicates going and he's shaky. He can't keep pyramiding forever." Drury stopped himself, and his face softened as his mind shifted from money matters. "But you're hardly interested in her financial problems."

"Oh, I don't know."

"Well, I'm not going to tell you. I was saying?"

"About this afternoon," Hank said.

"Oh, yes. I'll have lunch at the Poseidon and then go straight out to Raffneyville to see Marlin. I expect to stay overnight, too. No Sunday traffic for me. I'll come back tomorrow afternoon."

"Okay," Hank said. "I guess I can pick you up after lunch. But my radiator boils over and I may not be able to keep up with you."

"Why bother?" Drury said. "She's not coming with me, she said her house was too comfortable to leave, so you'll have nothing worth reporting. Hank, why not take the afternoon off? You might even stop in and see her."

Hank stared through the windshield and saw the shimmer of heat waves. Drury's suggestion was tempting and his reasoning sound. In decency to his conscience, Hank hesitated before he nodded consent.

"Well, I'll have to stop at the office first. A couple of things to do. Anyway, I'll wait for you to leave the restaurant," he said, taking out his pad. "And do you suppose you could stop for gas somewhere? If I can note down a detail like that, I'll feel better about the whole thing."

"Of course. I'll fill up at the crossroads station near Baker. I'll need a quart of oil, too. I'm low on it. You know the place I mean, don't you?"

"Mike Hanley's. Gulf. When do you figure you'll get there?"

"It's about an hour to the gas station, and then another half or three-quarters to Raffneyville. That should take care of any heavy traffic."

Hank nodded, opened the door and stepped reluctantly into the furnace blast.

He had lunch within sight of the Poseidon, and he could see Drury's car parked in the shade. Dawdling over a couple of sandwiches and some iced tea, Hank thought of Vivian in her air-conditioned sanctity, and he thought of what she'd said a couple of days ago. The gateway of the body. "You will know when," she had said.

He knew. Now.

Nevertheless he suspected that, in one way or another, her price would come high, for she was no ordinary woman. He could turn Jean on and off like a mercury switch and not even hear the click, but Vivian would be as sensational as the aurora borealis, and about as tameable.

When he saw Drury leave the restaurant at two-thirty, Hank slipped out to his car. To make sure Drury wasn't tricking him, Hank followed for a few blocks, towards Raffneyville. He kept out of sight and behind a couple of other cars. By the second traffic light he was convinced, and he turned and headed for his office, on the way to Vivian's. He could type out his report and then, with no more work on his agenda, he'd be free for the rest of the afternoon. And he'd relax at Lake Pride tonight, and return to the city late tomorrow.

Mike McGinty, the big, burly, Sunday watchman, unlocked the door of the Seagrave Building and greeted Hank warmly. Hank knew him from the parking lot days, when Mike had been a cop directing traffic at the nearest corner. He was slower and heavier now, and inclined to good-natured grumbling.

He muttered a complaint about the weather as he tramped across the empty lobby and picked up a clipboard for Hank to sign, as per routine, for nights and Sundays. But Hank hesitated, unwilling to place himself here, when he was supposed to be on the road to Raffneyville.

"Mike, any objections to letting me go up without putting my John Hancock on this?"

Mike, still holding the clipboard, frowned with doubt. "It's not that I don't trust you, Hank. But I've got my job to think of, and—"

"Skip it, then. All I need is my typewriter for a few minutes. You can bring it down."

Mike pulled at his jowls, and changed his mind. "Hell!" he said. "I'm not going to run errands for you. Come on, we'll forget about it." He shoved open the elevator door and stepped in.

Upstairs, the corridor was deserted. Room 1010 had Hank's name on it along with seven or eight others. He unlocked the door and stepped into the empty reception room. Libby Donneger wasn't at the switchboard to pucker up with her accordion smile and tell him that J. Edgar Hoover hadn't called today. Nobody was leaning over the steel files that belonged to the insurance agency from whom Hank sublet his tiny office, and no typewriters were clicking. His footsteps echoed somberly, as if he had no right to be there.

He unlocked the door of his office. It was just some space partitioned off into an area large enough for a secondhand desk, a secondhand leather chair, and a wooden filing cabinet. It fenced the air in nicely and kept it moist and motionless.

Hank sat down, slid the portable toward him, and rolled in a sheet of paper. He felt glued to the seat. He glared at the paper and, typing slowly, set down the routine information that concerned Drury.

"Left restaurant at 2.30 P.M., stopped for gas (Hanley's) about 3.30." It was harmless enough, but Hank reread it

38

carefully. Drury, he figured, ought to get to Raffneyville around four-fifteen.

The envelope stuck, from the humidity, and Hank worked the flap open and addressed it by hand. When the letter was sealed, he got up and went to the washroom. He doused cold water on his face, but he was sweating again before he'd even dried off.

Waiting for the elevator, he checked the collection schedule on the mail chute. No Sunday service, the letter wouldn't be picked up until nine A.M., Monday. Mrs. Drury would receive it Monday afternoon or Tuesday morning. By that time, the heat wave might be over.

He slid the envelope in the mailing slot and waited for Mike to take him down.

Outside, Hank climbed into his car and drove to Vivian's. He parked in the circle, next to a few other cars, and he stepped out. The maples shaded the sidewalk pleasantly, and the long high hedge seemed to absorb some of the blistering rays of the sun. Feeling like a kid going to a birthday party, he walked up the path to Vivian's house and rang the bell. There was no answer.

He stared at the grating that housed the speaker, and he rang again. He felt a quick, unreasonable anger. She should have known he was coming, she should have guessed it. Where was that sixth sense she bragged about?

He decided she was taking a nap, or else cooling off in a tub. He put his hand on the knob and turned it. The door opened. It had been open the other time, too.

In the coolness of the corridor, he stared at the blue madonna. He pursed his lips and wondered how Vivian felt every day when she looked at that picture. Beating herself over the head? Or had she simply stopped noticing it?

He shrugged, raised his voice. "Miss Vixen?"

Nobody answered. He shuffled his feet in annoyance and

remembered she'd told Drury she was staying home. Hank called again, loud and peremptorily. "Miss Vixen?"

There was still no answer.

He walked into the living room and approached the couch set on the dais in the corner. The pillows were piled invitingly and a green album lay face down near the foot of the sofa, as if she'd been in the middle of reading and had left for just a moment or two. He thought of the thousands of people who were sweltering, and it seemed to him that he had a sacred obligation to enjoy Vivian's air-conditioning.

He flung himself down on the lion skin. It was soft and luxurious, the mattress underneath was firm. He took his manual from his pocket, where he always kept it. The binding was shot and the pages were coming apart, and there was a crude drawing of a clown on the cover.

Hank smiled at it and remembered how he'd been studying one afternoon when Toby had come by and looked at the book. "What's that?" he had said.

"It's for grown-ups," Hank had answered. "No story. Just a lot of rules."

"Are there pictures in it?"

"No, nothing but words. And lots of long ones, too."

"Then make me a picture, Daddy."

Hank had sketched the clown, while Toby rubbed it with his finger, bursting into laughter, and then Hank hoisted him up on his knee.

The recollection of the scene reminded Hank that he'd promised to swim Toby, piggy-back, out to the raft. Frowning, Hank put the book down, picked up the album and saw the crumpled hankerchief that had been lying underneath it.

The album started with pictures of Vivian when she'd been at the height of her fame. The last section, however, showed Vivian after her accident, with her face toned down to indistinctness. In some of the pictures she was nude, in others she was costumed in the robes of a priestess, and finally there were a few where, in a manner of speaking, she was dressed, but in another manner she wasn't.

He closed the album. This was the Vivian who had spoken to him of the gateway to the body. She knew what she was talking about, too.

Hank stretched out and his feet hit the wall, smudging it. He stared at the smudge. Then, idly, he glanced around the room. An aperture in the wall indicated that there was a small projection-room behind the madonna portrait in the hall. A portable movie-screen was stacked against a chair. Something glittered on the carpet near it, and Hank got up to examine it. He found a highball-glass, not quite empty. The rug next to it was stained. He sniffed at the glass and smelled whisky.

He put the glass on the telephone-table and saw a pad with a notation. His own office phone number. Puzzled, he rubbed his chin. She'd wanted to get in touch with him, and she must have called today, Sunday. Otherwise he'd have gotten the message.

If she'd called.

Obsessed now with the feeling that something was wrong, he crossed the room and went into the kitchen. It was modern and had all the latest appliances. A bottle of eight-dollar whisky was open on one of the counters. He picked up the bottle, set it down. Then he opened the refrigerator.

The pitcher of orange juice appealed to him more than the whisky. He found a glass and filled it. He drank slowly, and when he finished, he started for the sink to rinse out his glass. Then he heard the front door open.

He called out, "Miss Vixen?" There was no answer, but he thought the door closed softly.

He called out again, "Hello?" He banged the glass down on the sink and strode to the front of the house. He opened the door, stepped out and marched down the path and out to the sidewalk. No one.

He turned slowly. What was there to worry about? Somebody comes to see Vivian and hears Hank yell. Probably doesn't even catch the words. So the guy leaves.

Or else he was still hiding in the garden. If so, it was too hot to look. With a shrug, Hank started up the path. Something caught at his trousers and there was a ripping sound. He bent down. A thorn had ruined his second-best pants. When he unhooked them he left a small sample on the thorn. He resumed his walk to the house and slammed the door behind him.

Inside, the madonna in blue gazed at him, but he was no longer impressed with her compassion. He kept thinking of the photographs in the album, and the angels drifting around the edges of the painting did not seem at all celestial.

He decided to have a look through the whole house, and then drive up to the country and have that swim with Toby. And the hell with waiting around for Vivian. At this rate he'd go crazy.

The living-room was on one side of the corridor, a closed door on the other. Whistling, he opened it. He saw Ron's picture on her bureau, and then he tripped over something, and he whirled. What he saw on the floor sent his heart hammering against his ribs with a tremendous thud, and the breath was almost slapped out of him.

Vivian Vixen was lying on the floor. She was dressed in her loose, white gown, and a fillet was tied around her head. The jeweled hilt of a dagger stuck at a lopsided angle from the circle of blood on her chest. A corsage of orchids had been fastened to her shoulder and had slipped off. The bent pin was still caught in the white, silk knot of her dress.

Hank uttered a sharp, guttural sound. It was the tripping over her that unnerved him. If he'd merely seen her, nothing more, he wouldn't have knocked himself out like this. He'd have taken it in his stride. Maybe.

She was dead, and he didn't have to examine her to be sure of it. Dead, dead, dead. Her eyes were glassy, her face was contorted and her mouth, finally ripped free of its stitches, was twisted, as if shrieking in perpetual silence. But she was like other people, no longer a freak.

42

There was only one thing to do. Call the police and report this. He turned, started for the telephone and then stopped.

If he called the police, what about his report? Every move of his would be investigated and checked. The police would find out that he'd gone to his office without signing-in, and that he'd given false information to a client. They'd lift his license, and there might be trouble about his civil-service exam.

That settled it. No mere murder was going to cheat him out of his chance for a civil-service job.

He was badly shaken as he returned to the bedroom and stood in the doorway, studying her. He didn't look at her face. Another face was embedded in his memory, the one he'd seen in the portrait out in the hall. Keep that image, don't let it go, that's the way to remember her. But study the dagger, the jeweled hilt that had an inscription.

He knelt down and saw that the writing was Arabic. It was the dagger he'd seen on the wall the other day. At least, he reflected, she'd been in character, theatrical to the end. A genuine Arabian blade, with jewels and an esoteric inscription. And orchids for her farewell.

He picked them up. They were bound in lavender-and-yellow ribbon, with printing on it. The ribbon was twisted so that he couldn't read it without taking the corsage apart.

He stood up, holding the orchids, and he walked back to the hall. He saw an orange vase on the table near the madonna portrait. He put the orchids in the vase and re-placed it on the table. Then he waited, with his hand in his pockets.

Nothing crossed his mind, and he told himself he'd better beat it, and fast. Then he heard the strange bumping, scratching sound, like the muffled thud of a rusty, metal leg.

He realized that somebody was outside and he was hear-ing the shuffle of feet on the bent, steel door mat, maybe a hand scraping the door frame—ordinary, matter-of-fact noises which the speaker-system translated into odd, un-nerving sounds.

43

For the space of two heart beats there was silence. Then a distant refrigerator clicked on, he heard the whir of the air-conditioner. The normal, routine machinery of the house beat at his ears. He waited for the door to open.

She came in swiftly and quietly. Her head was bent and her eyes were cast down, as if she was watching her feet execute a complicated ballet step. Two paces forward, extend right leg, swing it and turn with a click of the heels. Still concentrating on the floor, she took one further step forward. At the sight of Hank's shoes, she let out a gasp.

She raised her head slowly until her eyes, large and attractive and anxious, met Hank's. Her scared face, over-painted and framed by honey-colored bangs, was in shadow. Below it, the thin material of her yellow dress rose to the curve of her breasts.

He blinked. When he looked again, she seemed to have gotten over her fright. She was regarding him intently, and her wide, vermilion lips were parted in a beseeching oval, as if she was pleading with a kind of pitiful urgency. Please, don't laugh.

He shook his head. No. He wasn't going to laugh. He understood. She'd been practicing a role, something private between her and Vivian, and she hadn't expected to run into Hank. Now, she wanted to be herself again and to resume her dignity.

So he wouldn't laugh. But he had to get rid of her tactfully.

"Hello," he said. "Who are you?"

"I was looking for Vivian," she said in a hoarse, whispering voice.

"She isn't here."

"I'm sorry, I didn't mean to break in. That is—" She stopped in embarrassment. Her large, round eyes swept him and drifted past. He moved sideways to block off her vision to the bedroom.

"Sure," he said, trying to make it easy for her. "You didn't expect to find anyone. You expected to walk straight up to

44

the picture and look at it. And instead, you almost bumped into me."

"What are you talking about?" she asked in bewilderment.

"About Vivian's picture. The effect it has on people."

"Yes, but I came to see Vivian."

"She isn't here."

"You said that before." The girl was fighting him now, she resented his presence and resented the way he blocked off the corridor. "When do you expect her?"

"She won't be back."

"Oh."

It struck Hank that maybe the girl wanted to sit down and cool off for a while, she was waiting for him to invite her inside, and he wasn't going to.

"Were you just leaving?" she asked suddenly. "If she isn't coming back and you were here at the door—well, I don't want to keep you."

"No," he said. "I wasn't leaving."

He grinned, but his grin felt empty. He had set up an awkwardness, he'd created a situation instead of making light of it. He should have taken her by the arm and said, "She's not home, so come on out and let's cool off with some ice cream."

Except that he couldn't have done that, either. When the police investigated, they'd have a witness to place Hank here, at the house. He should have hidden and never let her see him, but it was too late now. He couldn't make her unsee him and he couldn't explain his predicament. He'd said words which, when repeated, would be damning.

He thought of opening the bedroom door and saying, "There, I found her and I'm in a spot and so are you."

But she wasn't. She was safe, because Hank had preceded her. And if she ever got into police hands, she'd make the most of it.

He narrowed his eyes, studying her and trying to catch the essence of her, seeking some character handle on which to turn his next move. She seemed alert, yet barely interested in him. Her glance darted around, taking in the bedroom door that was almost shut, the slice of living-room that was visible to her, the portrait, the ceiling, the table in the corridor.

Then she stopped her quick, restless examination and she fastened her eyes on something behind him. He turned to see what had caught her attention.

"Those orchids," she exclaimed. "I simply love orchids, I can't resist them. I'm sure Vivian won't mind." And, with a wide, satisfied smile, pleased that she'd finally hit on something to extricate herself from an embarrassing situation, she slipped past Hank and picked up the corsage.

"They're lovely, aren't they?" she said, pinning them to her dress. "Thank you."

Hank nodded helplessly. "Sure, take them, they look nice on you."

He swallowed, nodded too vehemently. But he was finally rid of her. She was leaving, she hadn't noticed anything wrong, she had no suspicions. She flashed him a final, self-conscious smile, opened the door and went out.

He heaved a deep sigh. Then, with businesslike efficiency, he proceeded to eliminate evidence that might be embarrassing to him. With particular attention to the album, he rubbed all places where he might have left fingerprints. He tore off the top page of the telephone pad, and removed as many more sheets as might conceivably hold a pencil impression.

He left as soon as he could, and once he was out of the neighbourhood, he did some careful thinking. Vivian Vixen's murder would be sensational and, since he'd followed her for about three months, he was bound to be questioned.

Thanks to Ron Drury, Hank had an alibi which was documented down to the detail of a stop for gas. But more to the point, the alibi worked both ways. Ron rather than Hank would be under suspicion. For Ron to state that at his own suggestion Hank had stayed in town—oh, no. Ron had to stay away from that line.

As for the presence of Hank's car in the parking-circle, he had slight worries. The car was inconspicuous, and citizens don't go around memorizing license numbers. And when they do, they're usually mixed up.

Mike would probably protect him on the office visit, too. There was no record, and Mike had to stand on that or risk his job. Besides, who was going to ask?

Which left the girl. If she spoke up, Hank was hooked; if she didn't, why would anybody even dream that he'd been at Vivian's? The question would never be raised.

He thought hard about the girl. The way she'd hesitated outside the house, and finally come in without ringing the doorbell. The way she'd never asked Hank who he was or what he was doing there. The more he analyzed her behavior, the more peculiar it seemed.

What it boiled down to, then, was a complete lack of reason to investigate Hank. Nobody, barring the girl, was likely to accuse him or involve him, which was a lucky break. Because, once the police spotlight focused on him, he'd be through.

He didn't let himself think about that. He glanced at his watch. Four o'clock. He marched boldly out of the house and went straight to his car. It started without trouble, and he took it down Bierce and headed for the highway. When he reached it, he held the car to a conservative forty. He'd get to the lake in time for a late swim with Toby.

Thinking of his son, Hank began to relax.

4

ON MONDAY MORNING, Mitch Taylor rode the bus to work. He climbed in and showed his potsy to the bus-driver and said: "Hot enough

47

for you?" The bus-driver said: "Yeah, going to be another tough one, but I knock off at the end of this run. Trouble is, I can't sleep in the heat."

"Yeah," Mitch said with feeling. "You get it in the neck, one way or the other."

He knew.

Nevertheless, he stood stalwartly, feet spread wide to brace himself against the movement of the bus, shoulders thrust back, with the top button of his nylon shirt taking the strain. He should have been a bus-driver, he told himself. Then they couldn't dock you or slap you down the ladder. Whatever your paycheck was you could count on it.

He thought of the good old days and that extra five hundred. But he missed the gang, too. He still saw Jub Freeman regular of course on account of Jub was his best friend. And with Jub married to Gladys, who used to work for the Homicide Squad, the Freemans and the Taylors were closer than ever.

Mitch supposed things could have been a lot worse. Oscar Henderson, who was his partner on patrol, wasn't a bad guy, although he wasn't exactly Mitch's type. Oscar was smart enough, but he was on the quiet side. His lips stuck out a little, like a fish, and he read a lot and had his mind mostly on pensions. But what he really went for was school-time when he could park the patrol car on a busy corner, step out and handle traffic. His face kind of lit up when the kids called him by his first name and the mothers said hello. And how, Mitch asked himself, could you make a buck out of that?

So here it was Monday morning, and Mitch got off the bus and went to the precinct and down to the locker-room to put on his uniform. He kidded around, and then he lined up while the squad got their orders and then he and Oscar went into the garage and took Number Seven-Four, same as always. They started out talking about the heat and then Mitch tried to switch over to some of the people in the precinct. When Oscar opened up, you never knew, he might give a lead you could use, if you worked it right.

But this morning all Oscar could think about was his silver wedding anniversary that was coming up in a few weeks, and what should he get for the wife. Then, at nine-eighteen, the two-way phone crackled, and Oscar picked it up.

"Henderson, Car Seven-Four." He listened and then said, "Vivian Vixen, Ten-Thirteen Bierce. Okay, Sergeant." He hung up.

"Her?" Mitch said. "What does *she* want?"

"Nothing," Oscar answered. "She's dead. So we go there and wait, until the Homicide Squad takes over."

"Huh?" said Mitch. He thought of that hundred bucks, and it hit him how lucky it was he hadn't taken it and maybe had her write his name down for a pay-off. "Huh?" he said.

In a kind of daze, he stepped on the gas, swung right on Whittier and jumped the next red light. He used the siren to cross Hawthorne and he hit Bierce at the four-hundred block. He shot straight down until he came to 1013. He parked in front of the hedge, snapped the door open and got out on the far side. He followed Oscar up the short path.

Inside the house, Mitch felt the air-conditioning and saw the Mother of God under blue lights, and he stopped short before he realized it was a painting. Then this cleaning woman began yapping at him, and he swung around and looked at her. Considering her age, maybe fifty or so, she had nice blue eyes, but the skin on her face was pulled tight, as if she was always trying too hard, worrying too hard, wanting what she couldn't get. Which was probably dough.

Anyhow, she talked too much. "I called you, I thought you'd never get here, it's just awful, I came in and I didn't even know. I started to work because that's what I always do and—"

"Where is she?" Mitch asked.

49

D

She pointed to the door off the corridor. "In there. I went in and—"

Mitch cut her off. "Let me have a look," he said.

He opened the door. He'd had plenty of training in homicide work and so he stood there, not going in, but looking at the body and then looking around and getting an impression before he took in the details.

Stabbed, with a knife that had a fancy hilt. Funny-looking nightgown on, and those rags around her head. No evidence of a scrap, nothing disturbed. Probably died quick, hooked the corner of the bedspread, and that was it. A fancy dress lying on the bed. A guy's picture on the bureau. Knife went in from the side and down, with plenty of force. Maybe the guy was standing behind her or maybe she turned into him when he let her have it. You couldn't tell which, but it explained the angle of the knife.

He closed the door. The maid was still talking about how awful it was, so he chopped her off.

"What's your name?" he asked.

"Martha Wayburn. I come in every morning at nine, except Sundays of course, and I clean up and there's always a note on the telephone-table telling me what time to wake her, only there was none this morning. 'That's funny,' I says to myself. Because she never forgot it before and I didn't know what to do, what time to knock on her door. I thought she might be sick and so I knocked and there was no answer and then—" She grabbed Mitch's arm and looked up in terror. "Mister, I never saw her before!"

Mitch gave her a look of disgust. "What do you mean?"

"It's Miss Vixen all right, I did see her, but I mean I never *really* saw her. She always had a veil on or was behind a screen or turned around in bed and was looking the other way. On account of her face."

"What's the matter with her face?" Mitch asked. "Looks like any face does, when it's dead."

"They say that's exactly the way it's always looked. Dead. She couldn't move it."

50

"Let's try and get this straight," Mitch said. "She didn't let people look at her, I know about that. Okay. So you came in. Did you clean up, disturb anything?"

"Oh, no, there wasn't time. I emptied the trash baskets and took the papers outside to burn. I always do that first, I like to watch fires."

"You do, huh?" said Mitch. Wait till Lieutenant Decker heard that one, all she'd done was burn up the papers, and half the time they were the best lead you were going to get. Mitch could almost see her out there with a poker, messing around and making powder out of the stuff, so that nobody would be able to reconstruct. Not even Jub, who was the best lab man in the business.

"Well?" Mitch said. "Then what?"

"Then I got out the vacuum cleaner and looked for her note, and then I knocked on her door and that's all."

Mitch coughed. This wasn't his job, all he was supposed to do was wait and see that nothing was touched until Lieutenant Decker and his gang took over. After that, they'd maybe send Mitch on some errand. So, before they got here—"

"About the knife," he said. And Martha pulled at his arm and brought him to the entrance of a room that looked like a Turkish harem without the harem around, and she pointed and said: "There! The dagger was always hanging on the wall, on that white spot. She kept it all those years, and it's fate, I say."

Mitch knew all about fate. Fate meant eating a lousy ham sandwich and then having a hood walk down an alley with nobody to knock him off. Fate was what usually happened to Mitch, and slapped him down just when he figured he had things under control.

But fate or not, he'd started Martha off, and she kept going. "When my husband was courting me," she said, "he used to say I looked like Vivian Vixen. But if I'd had her looks, the way she used to be, I mean, I wouldn't have married *him*. Not that he didn't do his best—"

51

"This dagger on the wall," Mitch said. "Any reason for showing it off like that?"

"Because of when she was making that movie in Africa, *Desert Princess*. There was a revival of it last year and I saw it, and she has pictures of herself with the same clothes on, and no wonder that Arab got notions. If she'd dressed respectable, it would never have happened. But he was intoxicated with her beauty."

"Who?" said Mitch, getting lost.

"The Arab who was working with her in the picture, and he had a horse. The Arabs, they like horses and they like women, and so he sneaked into her tent and tried to make love and she repulsed him. That's why he tried to stab her, but she screamed and fought him off until help came, and she kept the dagger all these years for a souvenir."

"Yeah," said Mitch. "Now look, Martha. My partner here, he wants your address and telephone number, see?"

He turned away. He had kind of an idea he'd like to case the joint, not touch anything, just look it over and maybe get an idea. You never know. So he sicked her onto Oscar and he crossed the room and stood in front of the raised couch stuck in the corner. He saw the cigarette-ash and the coaster, and he thought of a dame lying there, because that was what it seemed to be made for.

He noticed a big green album and he spotted the edge of a book that had slipped down between the mattress and the frame of the couch. So he reached down and picked up this book that was coming apart, and it was a manual for probation officers. And try to figure that one out.

He stepped back and examined the thing. The cover had a crude drawing of a clown. There was no name in the book, but some of the pages were marked and it had been read plenty, and not by a dame like Vivian Vixen. He still had the manual in his hand when Martha broke loose from Oscar, or maybe Oscar did it on purpose. Anyhow, there she was clacking away again, and Mitch didn't want her to see he'd picked up this book, so he went into the next room and stuffed it in his hip pocket alongside his guide to the city streets.

She was right behind him when he went into the kitchen, and he didn't have a chance to put the manual back without her or Oscar noticing. So he let it ride, he'd get rid of the book later on, no reason to let it bother him.

He was standing at the door when the boys came in. Decker, grim and serious and bristling with energy, blinked at sight of Mitch and almost broke his stride. He nodded curtly.

"Taylor," he said, as if Mitch meant bad news.

Mitch said, "Morning, Lieutenant."

Then Jub, breaking into his dimpled grin, said, "Hiya, Mitch," and the rest of the boys came in, kidding him like old times.

Mitch made like he didn't mind, but he was burned up inside. And the worst of it was those comfortable, fancy sport-shirts they were wearing, when here was Mitch with a collar and tie and a heavy uniform shirt that was made for Eskimoes. It was that, rather than the way they took over like they owned the place, which set Mitch thinking.

Suppose, for instance, he picked up something they missed, spotted some kind of a clue or figured something out, what would happen then?

Well, it had to be handled right. He didn't kid himself about this gang, either. They knew their business, they didn't pass up much. But, you take a big case, you have a whole bunch of leads and only eight guys on Homicide to run them down. So you pick the ones you're going to work on right off, and for a while you forget about the others, you can't bother with 'em. The lieutenant, he'd eventually get around to them and he'd do a better job than Mitch, Mitch didn't kid himself about that. But suppose it turned out that the less likely stuff hit bingo, and suppose Mitch had a little time on his hands and happened to pick up some information that didn't start off like a particularly good bet. Well, that way Mitch would be in on the ground floor.

53

So there was always a chance. And if Mitch had this information and kept it under his hat, say, until around the time the Commissioner and the papers were on the lieutenant's neck for not cracking the case, then maybe Mitch could promote a deal. Put Mitch back on the Homicide Squad.

He ran a finger under his collar. He knew Decker better than that. This was one shoo-fly that didn't make deals. If Mitch held anything out, he'd be on the carpet. And besides, only a rookie went to work on his own time and expected to crack a homicide.

So the hell with it. The way things happened was, something dropped in your lap without you even tried, and then you went ahead and made love to it. Still—a chance to get back on Homicide? At a five-hundred-buck raise?

He patted the manual in his pocket. He'd intended to put it back, but the way things had worked out, he just hadn't been able to.

Fate, huh?

He stopped dreaming about fate. Through the door to the bedroom he could see Jub taking pictures and the lieutenant measuring off distances. The boys started coming to the bedroom door to report the stuff they were turning up. The information Martha had spouted a little while ago, about Vivian Vixen's habits, about the dagger. Then there was a pitcher of orange juice left out of the refrigerator, along with an unwashed glass, and no lipstick on it, either. Perkins found her personal address-book with a bunch of names in it, mostly men. This was the raw material, mostly useless, that triggers off every case.

When the medical examiner arrived, Mitch let him in and had to make like an usher. "In here, Doc. This way."

Mitch heard the lieutenant grunt, "Hi, Doc." The doctor answered gruffly. "Hi, Bill. Big one, huh?"

"Big. You'll get on television, Doc, if you play your cards right."

The door closed, and the sounds that Mitch heard thereafter were meaningless. When the door opened, Decker spoke to Mitch.

"Taylor, take one side of the block and find out if anybody was seen coming in here yesterday afternoon, particularly between noon and four P.M. Check on any cars, strange or otherwise, that were parked near here. You." He spoke to Oscar now, for the precinct men took orders from the Homicide Squad, which had sole jurisdiction. "You, same thing on the other side of the street." The door closed.

Mitch spent an hour or so finding out either nobody had been home, or else they'd been locked in with their air-conditioners, with the shades down and the fans humming nicely. Still, Mitch made a few friends and let himself get talked into a couple of cups of coffee.

When he came back to the Vixen house, Decker and Jub and most of the gang had gone. Mitch gave his information to little Ed Balenky, who had squatted down on the couch, plugged in a telephone and was working in comfort. The smoke from his cigar polluted the atmosphere, but most of it got sucked in by the fan and so the air was more or less purified.

"What the hell are you doing, Ed?" Mitch asked. "Playing harem?"

Balenky took the cigar out of his mouth, wiggled his hips and flashed a broad, gold-toothed grin. "I'm in charge," he said. "The boys went back, they got plenty of leads, so they left me here to get her morning mail and hold the fort. No touch."

"What gives?"

"Guy named Drury. Ever hear of him?"

"No."

"Intimate friend of hers, lots of moolah, the number-one boy." Balenky lolled back, squinted. "Mitch, what the hell are you sweating about?"

Mitch made a face. "It's hot out."

55

"Relax, boy. Take your shoes off, make yourself to home."
He pointed to a large, green album at the foot of the couch.
"And take a look at some of those pictures. Say, you see that
dress of hers lying on the bed? New style, boy. W-neck."

Mitch snorted, picked up the album and began looking at
pictures. They made his eyes pop. "Say," he said, in his
hoarse, piping voice, "She was all right, huh?"

"Give you ideas?" Ed said, needling Mitch.

Mitch crossed the room and put the album down on a
table that had a few magazines piled on it. He fished for the
probation manual and it almost came apart, but he slipped
it under the album and turned around. His expression was
innocent.

"Make anything out so far?" he asked.

"Kind of early," Balenky said, "but the lieutenant's talking
to Drury right now. He's *it*, Mitch. If he didn't do it he
knows all about her."

"The funny thing is," Mitch said, "it looks like this guy
took the dagger down from the wall and went into the bedroom and let her have it, just like that. No build-up, no sign
of a scrap. And things don't happen that way."

"The autopsy might show something," Balenky said.

"You mean, did somebody make love to her," Mitch said.
"Right here on the couch. Which is maybe why she put that
cigarette down and let it burn." He noticed the ash-tray was
gone and he said, pointing, "What happened to it?"

"Jub took it."

"What for?" Mitch asked, puzzled. "What the hell can a
cigarette ash tell him?"

"Nothing, but she was fixing her nails, she'd filed them
down on one hand and started on the other and never
finished up. The filings were dumped into the ash-tray and
maybe some of them spilled on the couch. That's what Jub's
working on, first. He'll be back later on to go through this
shack."

"Drury a big guy?" Mitch asked. Balenky didn't answer
and Mitch pointed to the smudge on the wall, near the foot

56

of the bed. "You got to be big for your feet to reach down there. Any idea when those marks were made?"

"This Martha, she says they weren't there Saturday. That's about as far as you can get. Look, Mitch—the lieutenant said when your partner gets through, he stays here but you can go down to the telephone company for the Vivian Vixen phone records. They got 'em all ready for you."

"Sure," said Mitch.

He went over and picked up the green album, as if for one more look, and then he appeared to notice the manual.

"What's that doing, around here?" he said, holding it up.

"Never noticed it," Balenky said. "Let's have."

Mitch handed him the book and Balenky examined it, frowning, like he couldn't read too good. "I'll show it to the boss," he said. "He didn't mention it."

"Yeah," Mitch said, feeling virtuous.

He was an errand-boy the rest of the day. Still, going in and out of headquarters, he picked up a little more information than they had on the radio or in the papers.

He knew, for instance, that Drury was a little guy and he'd started out as the chief suspect and ended up as the chief mourner. It seemed that his wife had hired a private eye named Greenleaf to follow him, and yesterday this Greenleaf had picked Drury up at noon and stayed on his tail until four-fifteen.

Mitch happened to be around when Perkins came in after checking on how Drury'd stopped for gas. Drury hadn't mentioned it but Greenleaf had, and so Perkins went up and even got the charge-slip, sixteen gallons and a quart of oil.

The Raffneyville police had checked up on Drury. The cook said he'd arrived at four-fifteen and then gone down to the village for a while. There, he had the mayor for an alibi, and that just about cleared Drury, and now he and the lieutenant were palsy-walsy and Drury was helping out all he could. As for Greenleaf, yesterday he'd been riding around all over the map. Up to Raffneyville and then all the way back to Lake Pride, where his family was staying.

The lieutenant had a list of Vixen's boy friends, and he lined them up outside his office like he was selling tickets to the world series. They all started out saying they were acquaintances of hers, were interested in her philosophy, but none of them had much of an idea what it was. They threw big words around and told how wonderful she was and how she preached you should love everybody, including yourself.

The lieutenant didn't buy that, the way they used the word *love*, it meant just one thing to him, and by and by they all got around to agreeing with him. It seemed she threw these parties and they started out like a poetry society, and once or twice they ended up that way and everybody went home like little gentlemen. But what happened the other times, the lieutenant kept to himself, on account of all he was interested in was homicide and collecting a few alibis. Which he got all right.

These boy friends, he checked them off like he was running them through an IBM machine. Most of them had too much dough to hang around the city on a Sunday. They'd gone swimming or else were sitting in the country clubs playing bridge, and so far there wasn't anybody you could even hang a misdemeanor on. Which soured the lieutenant but didn't bother Mitch at all. It wasn't his worry, this trip.

Around four he managed to make himself scarce, so he went up to the precinct and checked out, called Amy and gave her the story and that was Mitch's day. No pressure, no overtime work. Now, he was free to knock off and go home.

Amy had the kids down in the garden of the apartment house where the Taylors lived. Somebody was watching them, and Amy was in halter and shorts, fussing around the kitchen and making iced tea. Somehow she reminded him of well water or a brook with not too much sun on it. Just looking at her gave Mitch a lift, and he kissed her hard and then pulled away.

"Me for a shower," he said. "How do you keep cool like that, Amy?"

She laughed. "I have a new trick. I took the children shopping."

"Huh?" he said.

"The stores are air-conditioned," she explained. "Mamie and Joey love it, they look at the toys. I explained they had to hold hands and not touch anything, and they were good as gold."

"You got more nerve than me," he said. "But what do you do—walk around all day?"

"Oh, no. We have a sort of club, a few of us meet there and we sit at counters and pretend we're going to buy, and then we get interested in talking to each other and the salesgirls don't bother us. Sometimes one of us really does buy. And, sometimes I pick up useful information."

Mitch stretched out in a chair and took his shoes off. "Like what?"

"Well, I met Jean Fergus this morning, she came into town to get some things for this detective's little boy. Toby Greenleaf. Of course, I didn't know who he was then."

"Oh. The guy that was on Drury's tail."

"Yes, Mr. Greenleaf drove her in from the country this morning. Toby and Mamie just love each other. He's her first boy friend."

Mitch chuckled at the idea of a couple of five-year olds hitting it off.

Later on, after he'd had his shower and after the kids had come upstairs, Mamie sat on his lap and squirmed, until she got interested in pulling at the hairs on his chest.

"I hear you got a sweetheart," he said.

Mamie nuzzled up to him. "Daddy's my sweetheart, but I like Toby, too."

Mitch laughed. "Hey, Amy, I got competition. A younger guy, he's cutting me out."

Amy smiled. "You'll have to fall back on me."

Mamie tugged at another hair, and Mitch said "Ouch!"

Mamie studied him attentively. "You know what?" she said.

"What?"

"Toby can swim. He swam way out to the raft, and it's miles and miles."

"All alone?" Mitch said, amused.

"No, on his daddy's back. His daddy can swim miles and miles, too."

"When did all this happen?"

"Yesterday," Mamie said. "When his daddy came home. Then Toby sat on the raft for a long time and got sunburned, I saw the blister. Then he had to go home and cook supper."

"Toby, he does the cooking?" Mitch said.

"Because, he doesn't have a mother," Mamie announced, in utter seriousness.

Mitch didn't go into Mamie's logic, which was some kind of a mix-up about mothers being cooks, and when they weren't there you had to do the cooking yourself. What stuck in Mitch's mind was, how this Greenleaf got back from Raffneyville in time to have a swim and then loaf around on the raft, all before supper.

So Mitch got up and pulled out some road maps and began studying them. Raffneyville, where Greenleaf was supposed to be at four-fifteen, was a good hour and a half from the city, and Lake Pride was another hour and a half in the other direction. Figure Sunday traffic and the detour where the new, belt highway wasn't finished, and you'd have to go by helicopter to make Lake Pride before seven-thirty. And at seven-thirty there wasn't much sun, you couldn't get a blister. And besides, it was kind of late to take a kid swimming.

So either little Toby was a liar, or else there was something screwy.

Amy noticed that Mitch didn't talk much at dinner. She said once, "Tired?"

"Me?" said Mitch. "The heat don't knock me out like that."

Amy circled to behind his chair, put her arms over his shoulders and kissed the top of his head. "I know," she said in a soft, low voice. "It's being left out of it."

"Yeah," said Mitch.

"I asked Gladys to drop over with Jub, later on."

"Jub won't come, he'll be working till midnight, at least. This is big stuff, Amy. The reporters are all over head-quarters and one of the big-shot radio guys, he flew in all the way from New York."

Amy's cheek brushed Mitch's ear, lightly. "Decker will need every man he can use. And he knows you're good."

"Don't dream," Mitch said. "It's no fun waking up." He separated her arms, pushed his chair back and stood up. He rolled his shoulders under his white, nylon sport-shirt.

"I got to see a guy about something," he said. "I may be a while."

He went out. No sense telling Amy about it, this was a long shot if there ever was one. Still, he had a funny feeling he'd hooked onto something. This Greenleaf could have turned himself around after Drury had gassed-up at Baker, and then he could have stopped off at a little white house on Bierce.

In which case, Greenleaf, he was Mitch's boy.

5

WHEN HANK STROLLED down to Mario's (Bar and 50c. Pizzas) on Monday evening, he left word at his apartment.

Just in case.

He'd seen her sitting in an anteroom at headquarters as he'd passed through, early in the afternoon. Her honey-colored hair, combed smooth and straight, fell in a low wave on her forehead. Her legs were crossed at the knees, and her ankles were intertwined. Leaning forward, with her lips parted in an easy smile, she seemed completely at home.

The detective alongside her was talking with an air of casual friendliness, that probably concealed a driving ambition to make her by sundown.

For an instant, Hank thought he'd get by without being noticed. Then she turned her head. Her pale eyes, still twinkling with amusement, widened slowly and grew limpid. She said to the detective, "Who is he?"

Hank kept on walking. He heard the detective answer, "Him? Greenleaf, a private investigator. Why? Know him?"

The drawl of of her voice carried to the door as Hank stepped out. "No," she said. "But I'd love to."

Then he was in the corridor. Still free. A little shaky. Wondering what she'd meant. Deciding he might hear from her before the day was over. She knew his name, she could look him up in the phone book, she could get in touch.

Jean and Toby had come in with Hank early this morning, ostensibly on a shopping trip to outfit Toby. But that was merely an excuse, as Hank realized almost as soon as he got behind the wheel of the car. Jean's real reason was that Hank was slipping through her fingers, and she wanted to show him what a tight little family they'd make.

In the car, she began talking about the Taylors, but Hank hardly listened. He gave her an occasional appraising glance. He saw an attractive girl with black, crinkly hair and dark, lively eyes. She had one arm around a restless, chattery Toby. Between wriggles he kept grabbing her dress to hoist himself up. Every time he pulled at it he exposed her shiny brown thighs, and she uttered an embarrassed little laugh. "*Please*, Toby," she said. "Please."

Then Hank said, "Be a good guy, Toby. I need you to help drive." Immediately Toby grabbed at the steering wheel, and Hank pushed him back. "I didn't mean that, Toby. You know you're not supposed to bother the driver. Play with Jean a while, huh?"

"Daddy, can't Jean come live with us all the time?"

Hank managed to laugh, but it sounded hollow. "Maybe she doesn't want to," he said gruffly. And Jean, not daring to

62

look at Hank, gave Toby a quick hug and said, "Oh, Toby—how can you!"

Hank figured he should have proposed to her then and there, for his own sake as well as Toby's. Even if he wasn't in love with her, she had her rights and he was willing to admit she'd make a pretty good wife. Sex and companionship, and a mother that Toby liked. What more could Hank ask for, anyhow?

Not love. He'd had love once and he'd seen it rot at the center. Maybe a sensible arrangement with a sensible girl was a lot better. She was female, she wanted him. He was male, and he wanted somebody. Why fight?

He switched on the radio. "News," he said.

He kept it on, waiting hopefully for the flash about Vivian Vixen. It didn't come.

After he'd left Jean and Toby near a department store and made arrangements for meeting them in the afternoon, Hank went to his office. He was the first to arrive, and he unlocked his cubicle and sat down at his desk. He waited until shortly after nine, when the buzz and hum of the day had started. Then he stepped out to the reception-room.

Libby Doneger looked up from the switchboard and greeted him with a grin she must have saved up all weekend. "Oh, Hank—good morning. I didn't know you were here."

"Got in early," he said. "I had some reports to type and I wanted them to make the first collection. I mailed them a half-hour ago. Have a good weekend?"

"I spent the day in an air-conditioned movie, and I met the nicest man in the lounge. We saw the picture through twice, and simply gorged on popcorn."

"You must have been hungry," Hank said. "I'm on my way out. Any messages, I'll call back, but I'm not sure when."

"Are you after those Russian spies again?" she said, in a stage whisper.

"No. This time they're after me."

He went downstairs and crossed the street to the lunch

counter where they kept the radio going all day. He ordered crullers and coffee, and sat down in a booth where he could listen. After a while, he fished in his pocket for the manual.

With a shock, he realized he didn't have it. He sat stiffly, trying to remember.

He'd had it when he'd stretched out on Vivian's couch, and he couldn't recall seeing it since. He began feeling jittery, and he thought of how a good investigator could tie Hank up to that manual.

There was his habit of carrying it around with him, and his inability to produce it. Pencil marks, ink marks, doodlings. He might have scribbled down his name without realizing it. His fingers had touched every page, and he wondered how many latent prints remained, waiting for a sprinkle of black powder to bring them out.

Buy another copy, he told himself, and claim you threw the old one away. Don't buy another, forget you were ever interested in probation work. Get a civil-service list and start studying something else. Some kind of investigation. That ought to be easy for him.

He sat there in uncertainty, waiting for the news-flash about Vivian Vixen.

It came at ten o'clock. Just the simple announcement, no details. Hank listened, then got up, paid his check and went out. He wasted about an hour, which seemed like a reasonable time within which people might hear the murder had occurred. Then he went into a phone booth, called the Drury number and asked for Mrs. Drury.

"Have you heard?" he asked.

"Yes, isn't it awful? They'll have to question Mr. Drury, won't they?"

"Naturally."

"Did you see him yesterday?"

"Sure. My report's in the mail, you'll get it later on. I had him in sight from about twelve o'clock on. He had lunch and then drove straight out to Raffneyville."

64

"Thank God!" she exclaimed. "You'll tell the police, won't you?"

"I'm going over there now."

Hank had a lengthy wait in a side-room before he was allowed to see Decker. The lieutenant was sitting in a squeaky chair, and his small office was crowded with stacks of magazines, unfiled papers and other evidence of overwork. He looked like an owl when he was silent and like a woodpecker when he wasn't. He listened to Hank's story of having been hired to follow Drury and of having followed him yesterday. When Hank had finished, Decker spoke crisply.

"Let's see your identification."

Hank handed the lieutenant his license.

"You say you had him in sight all the way out?" Decker asked.

"On and off. I didn't stay too close, but I managed an occasional look."

"Traffic heavy?"

"Usual Sunday stuff," Hank said, as vaguely as possible.

"And what time did he gas-up?"

"About three-thirty, at Hanley's place."

"When Drury stopped, could you see him? Did he get anything besides gas?

"He had the hood up," Hank said, "and somebody came out with a can. Oil, I guess, although I was too far away to see clearly."

Decker made a notation, returned Hank's identification. "Ever speak to Miss Vixen?"

"No." Hank knew he was taking a chance, but to admit knowing Vivian was a subtle form of hari-kari. "I've been observing her for about ten weeks, but only in the course of watching Drury."

"This alibi you're giving him for yesterday afternoon," Decker said, studying Hank intently, "because that's what it is, he couldn't have a better one, if true." Hank raised his hands in a what-can-I-do-gesture, and Decker went on. "Got your report in writing?"

65

E

"I mailed it early this morning," Hank said.

"You have a carbon? And of all the others, too?"

"Naturally, but they're confidential."

"Confidential, my eye!" Decker said. "In fact, my private eye!" He leaned back and burst into uproarious laughter that got Hank and set him off, too.

The lieutenant thumped forward on his swivel-chair with a jolt that snapped his laughter like a cut wire. "Couple of prize dopes," he said, "laughing over a corny one like that. Now tell me about Drury and Vixen. What their relationship was, how they got along together, the gist of what you learned from watching them."

Hank told. When he was through, Decker asked Hank no questions about himself. There was no reason to, and Hank hoped there never would be. Then he went out and saw the girl.

He returned to his office and went to work re-establishing contacts and trying to drum up some new business. With Vivian dead, his paycheck was gone, too.

Around half-past three, he received a phone call. He recognized the voice at once, but he pretended not to.

"Yes?" he said. "Who's this?"

"I think you know. I just wanted to say I didn't mention seeing you."

"Good. We weren't there, either of us."

"Oh, thank you," she said, with obvious relief.

"Now that that's settled, who are you and when can I see you?"

She laughed softly. "I'm me, and I'd be scared to see you."

"No reason for that," Hank said. "I'll be home tonight, or else at Mario's bar. On Melville near Thoreau."

"Oh, no!" she said, and she hung up.

In the afternoon, he drove Jean and Toby back to the country. Jean was full of gossip and small adventures. She'd met Amy Taylor and they'd shopped together. Amy had two children, a little girl who was Toby's age and a three-year old boy, and Toby and the girl got along famously.

Presently, Jean ran out of steam. "You're so silent," she said. "And so preoccupied. What did you do today?"

"Had a session with the Homicide Squad, on the Vivian Vixen case."

"Hank!" she exclaimed in alarm.

"Nothing to worry about. I'd been doing some work that involved her, so I told the police what I knew."

"Tell me, too."

"I was trailing Drury. That's all."

"Yesterday?"

"Yes. And—" Hank glanced at her and gave her a quick smile. "Listen, Jean. If anybody should happen to ask, if the matter ever comes up, say that I didn't get to the lake last night until eight. And tell Dad, too. Eight o'clock, no earlier."

"Of course," she said. Her voice had a tender note, as if she was glad of the chance to commit a small sin for him. "You can count on me."

He turned and saw her eyes resting on him. She lowered them immediately and said, pointing: "Hank, did you know you have a tear in your trousers?"

He'd forgotten about that. He said, "Oh, yes. Caught them on a bush this morning. Luckily it's an old suit, I'm due for a new one, anyhow."

"It looks all right to me," she said. She paused and added slowly, "You know, I do remember your tearing it, but I don't recall exactly where."

"Neither do I," he said.

"Let me see, let me see," Toby said suddenly. "Ooh! Daddy!" And he squirmed down to get a better look.

So Hank, sitting there at Mario's, felt reasonably safe. He'd accounted for the rip, and for the postmark on his report. He'd gotten by the Homicide Squad, he'd learned that the girl had her own reasons for not admitting her presence at Vivian's, and he'd covered himself on the time schedule from Raffneyville to the bungalow at Lake Pride. Not a bad day's work, considering.

He ordered a beer and nursed it at a table which had the

door in sight. He half expected the girl to show up. She'd come in with that flat, graceful walk, and her large, pale eyes would seek him out. Then he'd stand up, and she'd break into a smile and come over to him. He wondered whether she'd be wearing the orchids.

Around half-past eight, a stocky, dark-haired guy in a white, nylon shirt with short sleeves ambled through the door. When he spotted Hank, he strode straight to the table and said, "Hello, Greenleaf. Mind if I sit down?"

Hank answered pleasantly enough. "Sorry," he said, "but I'm waiting for somebody."

"That's okay," the stocky guy said. "She'll keep."

He spoke with a cold, deliberate contempt, and with a brittle disregard for Hank. Hank felt his stomach knot up, and he grabbed the edge of the table.

"Beat it," he said in a low, angry voice. "I don't know you and I don't want to."

"You will." The guy pulled out a chair and sat down. "The name's Taylor. Police."

Hank stared. This was the guy Jean had been raving about. The model husband. Holier-than-thou. And he turned out to be son of a bitch who needed a kick in the teeth.

"Get out before I throw you out," Hank said, smoldering.

"You won't throw me out. I'm a cop."

"So what?"

"So we're going to have a little talk," Taylor said.

Hank snorted. He hated Taylor the way he'd hate a rattlesnake crawling across his living-room. And maybe for the same reason. Hank was scared.

With the admission, he saw that Taylor was deliberately needling him and wanted to get him worked up. Therefore, Hank gritted his teeth and held himself in tight control.

"All right," he said in a clipped voice. "If you got anything to say, let's hear it."

"The thing is," Taylor said, "you want to be careful. Just because you got away with it so far, you don't want to have ideas. Them shoo-flies fool easy."

"What are you raving about?" Hank demanded.

Taylor swung around in his chair and spoke to the bartender. "Mac, can I get a beer over here?" Then he turned back and faced Hank.

"I'll lay it right on the line for you, Greenleaf. You went swimming at Lake Pride yesterday. What time?"

Hank lifted his beer glass and said in a clipped tone, "I don't know whether to drink this or throw it in your face."

"Drink it," Taylor said, "and then tell me what time."

Hank said, "What business of yours—"

He broke off. Words wouldn't help, getting sore wouldn't help. He had to be smarter than this guy opposite him, he had to study the guy and understand him.

Hank leveled his gaze at Taylor. A face with health and energy, no lines. Strong enough lips, but neither hardness nor softness to them, as if the guy hadn't grown up, yet. Dark brown eyes that were unexpectedly soft, they fooled you.

The beer came and Taylor tasted it. "Let's you and me do a little thinking," he said. "How long would you say, for instance, it took to get from Raffneyville to Lake Pride?" He took a pencil and a scrap of paper from the pocket of his shirt. "Let's get it down, Greenleaf. You good at arithmetic?"

Hank shoved back his chair and stood up angrily. Through the open door to the street, he saw a girl with honey-colored bangs approach the entrance, hesitate. Then, noticing Hank was with somebody, she turned quickly and walked away. Taylor twisted around, but he was apparently too late to see the girl, and he made no mention of her.

"Not leaving," he said, "are you? Because I wouldn't, Greenleaf. I'd listen, first."

"To what?"

"Sit down and I'll tell you."

"You lousy bastard," Hank said. But he sat down.

"Thanks," Taylor said. "Now I'm going to come clean with you. I found that manual of yours, all beat up and coming apart, and with the pages marked up."

"I don't know what you're talking about."

"It was stuck down in the mattress of the couch. How come you forgot about a thing like that?"

"You say you found a manual of some kind," Hank said. "Is that right?"

"Yeah. Probation stuff. Picture on the cover, looks like a clown, but you don't draw too good. So now you know where we stand, huh?"

Hank didn't answer.

"Suppose," Taylor continued, "I knew it was yours, but nobody else did. Then what?"

Hank tried to figure this out. If Jean had told Amy Taylor about that manual, he was sunk. But he couldn't believe Jean was that dumb. Which meant Taylor was bluffing.

Hank said, "You're telling me you found a piece of evidence, that you concealed it, and you think it belongs to me."

"Hell, no!" said Taylor. "I wouldn't conceal evidence. I turned it over to Homicide, they got it. But they don't know the manual is yours, and I do. That's the thing."

"You claim something belongs to me, and it doesn't. Taylor, do you get these hallucinations often?"

"Don't kid yourself," said Taylor. "This ain't no dream. The thing is, I'm trying to give you a break. I picked up a little extra information and I'm telling you about it."

"Shakedown?" Hank demanded.

Taylor looked surprised. "Me?" he said. "Look, this is just a precinct investigation. The Homicide boys take the big shots, and the precinct checks up on stuff they can't bother with."

"Don't give me that," Hank said. "I know the set-up in this town. The Homicide Squad has jurisdiction, and you haven't. And right now, you're about as far off-base as you can get."

"That's right," Taylor admitted amiably. "But suppose I walk into Decker's office and say, 'Lieutenant, you want to check into this guy Greenleaf a little more careful, there's something funny about him. Because how could he take an afternoon swim at Lake Pride when he was all the way over in Raffneyville at four-fifteen?' You want me to do that, or you want to sit here and talk?"

"What I really want," Hank said, "is to step outside with you and find the nearest empty lot."

"No sense to that," Taylor said. "One of us would get hurt. Now suppose I could show you were a little hot in the pants about Vixen. That wouldn't look too good for you, would it?"

Hank scowled, picked up his beer glass and finished it. Taylor said, "You like beer, Greenleaf. What made you take orange juice yesterday? There was plenty of beer on ice."

"What's your badge number?" Hank asked crisply. "You say you're a cop, but how do I know?"

"You know,' Taylor said, "so why don't you quit boxing around? There's this swim you took at the lake—"

"Sure," said Hank. "I got back to Lake Pride around eight and had myself a swim. You can check on that."

"I did just that, but there's something fishy about it. Because how did that manual of yours get lost on the couch, huh?"

Hank made no reply. Clearly, once the manual was ident-ified as his, he was through. So Taylor was guessing, but it was a good guess, and it hurt. Hank decided to play it dumb, and he got up and went to the bar. He ordered another beer and carried it back to the table. He sat down and took a sip.

"Thinking things over?" Taylor said. "Well?"

"I'm thinking," Hank said slowly, "that you refused to show me a badge, that you're trying some roundabout extortion, and that if I go to your boss you'll be in trouble, and I won't."

"You're in trouble now," Taylor said flatly. "Did I tell you that the angle of the knife shows a tall guy killed her?" Taylor cocked his head and studied Hank coolly. "Someone about your height, I'd say."

"And what *you* say, that ties it up. They all listen to you, from the Commissioner down."

Taylor went right on, unbothered. "So this tall guy was lying on the couch, his feet were too long for it and they rubbed up against the wall."

"If you got so much evidence," Hank snapped, "why in hell don't you swear out a warrant and get it over with? What are you horsing around for?"

"I'm thorough," Taylor said modestly. "I figure you and me, we're going to stay with this till we get somewhere."

"You got as far as you're going. Your next step is out. Through that door."

Taylor looked offended. "Keep your shirt on," he said. "We got a lot of ground to cover. Now suppose, for instance, someone had been tailing Vixen for a couple of months. He'd have a lot on her, wouldn't he? The guys she slept with, those parties she gave, stuff like that. If he threatened to spill some of that dirt, there'd be kind of an argument, wouldn't there? And arguments like that, people lose their heads, they hardly know what they're doing." Taylor examined Hank attentively. "Got quite a temper, haven't you?"

Hank merely smiled. Without speaking, he rose, picked up his beer glass and walked over to the bar. He planted himself on the stool and began talking to the bartender.

About a minute later, he heard Taylor's footsteps approach the bar. Taylor said, "What do I owe you, Mac?"

Hank turned and watched Taylor accept his change and leave no tip. His face was expressionless when he spoke to Hank.

"Good night," he said. "I'll be seeing you, huh?"

6

THE WAY HANK
saw things in the cool, clear light of the next morning, he was like a man swimming the breaststroke in shark-infested

waters. The sharks weren't interested in him yet, but they were bigger than he was and they could swim better. Scratch him somewhere and bring out a little blood, and they'd swoop.

Three people could scratch him. Mike, who'd seen Hank at the office on Sunday afternoon. The girl, who'd seen him at Vivian's. And Drury, who knew Hank had faked his report. The gamble was whether Taylor would question any of them. And whether, if he did, they'd stand up under the pressure.

Taylor had used the octopus technique last night, and he was an expert at it. Try everything you can think of, tie a guy into knots and put him on the defensive and then blind him with an inky mass of slopped-up guesswork.

Hank, making breakfast in the kitchenette of his small apartment, decided he'd pulled a boner. He'd let Taylor get him mad.

Hank should have laughed it off. How could Taylor know when Hank had gone swimming? Probably someone had seen him at a distance, but if Hank denied being there and Jean backed him up—

Hank wondered, then, about Toby. The kid had been looking forward to that trip to the raft, it was a big thing in his life, he wouldn't forget it. He'd sat dead center on the raft, the way Hank had ordered him to, and he'd looked up into the sun and let it pour down and the laughter spill out, while Hank told him he'd be a champion swimmer when he grew up.

So Toby had probably told everybody about his long-distance swim, and Taylor might have heard about it. In which case Hank merely had to point out the absurdity of believing a five-year-old. When a kid wants something badly enough and his father promises it, the promise can replace the fact. A child's world is a hazy land of wishing and wanting, it's peopled by giants who turn bewilderingly from good to bad. Dreams and reality merge; anything can happen and usually does.

Easy. Make a liar out of your son, knock out his self-confidence, twist him around your finger and convince him he's all mixed up. You're bigger than he is, take advantage of it. Save your own neck.

Hank shook his head. He'd keep Toby out of this. The kid had enough problems, and Hank owed him the decent home life which a steady job would bring about. Except that now, Hank couldn't even file for his civil-service exam without the risk of tying himself into the Vixen case.

He began worrying about his false report and what would happen if the facts came out. At the best, he'd lose his license and he'd fumble around helplessly, with no earning power and not much chance of a job. At the worst, he might be charged with murder.

Basically, Hank had started the whole mess at the moment he'd dropped his letter to Mrs. Drury down the mail-chute. From then on he'd been a victim of bad luck. But why had Taylor latched onto him?

Taylor, who was mean and unscrupulous and shrewd, had been conducting no official investigation last night. He'd been on his own, and he'd handed out a bunch of threats, insinuations and accusations. What for?

Not for extortion. You put the bite on somebody who can really pay off. So Taylor had to have something else in mind, thus far unknown.

Hank grimaced. The only way to handle a guy like Taylor was to get something on him, and use it. Hit back hard.

After breakfast, Hank bought the morning papers, took them to his apartment and studied them. The Vivian Vixen case was headlined, with plenty of pictures and a souped-up story of her life, accent on the episode of the dagger. The police, however, weren't handing out much in the way of information.

Mr. and Mrs. Ronald Drury, as well as a number of other people, unnamed, had been questioned. The only item of importance that Hank learned was that Vivian Vixen had had an assignation with a man on Sunday, and that she had been making preparations to receive him. The police had clues to his identity, and were working on them.

Hogwash, Hank decided. They had no idea who the guy was, but they'd go all out to find him.

A half-hour later he walked into headquarters and spoke to the sergeant at the main desk.

"Rudy Myers, in the Records Bureau," Hank said. "Okay to go up and see him?"

"You know him?"

"Sure. Tell him Hank Greenleaf's here."

The sergeant, measuring Hank's poise and his big, athletic frame, nodded. "Room 217. Go on up."

Rudy, a deep-voiced guy with a beer-and-pretzels face, was bent over paper work. When he saw Hank he straightened up, pushed over a chair with his good leg and said, "Long time no see. Still making a buck out of divorce stuff?"

Hank shook hands and sat down. "A buck is right. What's with you, besides a few extra pounds?"

Rudy grunted. "I don't get no exercise. I sit here with a bullet in my leg, and I accumulate." He liked the word and he repeated it. "I accumulate."

Hank laughed, and for the next few minutes they exchanged news and brought each other up to date. Then Hank said, "Rudy, I wonder if you can do me a favor. Know a cop named Taylor, working out of the Fourteenth?"

"It wouldn't be Mitch Taylor, would it? Used to be on Homicide."

"I didn't know about the Homicide. He's a stocky guy, dark hair, dark eyes, high-pitched voice. And plenty of nerve."

Rudy's chuckle made his chair vibrate. "That's him all right. What's he up to now?"

"He's riding me, for some reason I can't figure. I'd like to get a line on him."

"Comes from New York," Rudy said. "He was in the New York department and moved out here around the same time as Jub Freeman, the lab wizard. They pal around together, and Taylor landed on Homicide. But he never got along with Decker, he was always in Decker's hair. Then a couple of months ago they had this gunman in a trap and Taylor let him walk through. His boss hit the ceiling. That's why Taylor got dumped, and shipped out to the Fourteenth. Wait a minute, Hank. Let me see if there's anything else."

Rudy stood up and hobbled over to a filing cabinet. He pulled out a drawer, rummaged for a couple of minutes and then limped back.

"He's got one citation, a couple of years back," Rudy remarked. "I remember for a while we thought he was the Commissioner's boy, he was up in the Commissioner's office a few times and they'd stop and talk in the hall. Then something happened and the Commissioner dropped him."

"He was broken, though?" said Hank.

"Transferred, is all it says. There's nothing against him on the record, but it speaks for itself. An inspector on the Homicide Squad, and then a uniformed patrolman. That's a difference of a few hundred bucks a year."

"What was the name of this gunman?"

"Nolan. Spike Nolan. The troopers finished him after he shot up a gas station."

"And this business with the Commissioner," Hank said. "Any idea what was behind it?"

Rudy shrugged. "I wouldn't know. Taylor plays the angles, and I'm just giving you the scuttle-butt. But I'd be careful, Hank. Don't underrate Mitch Taylor, he usually lands on top." The curves in the pretzel-face deepened. "Has he got anything on you?"

Hank shook his head. "No, but he's trying." He stood up, dropped a hand on Rudy's basketball of a shoulder and said, "Thanks, Rudy. Maybe I can make him sweat a little."

"Yeah," Rudy said. He didn't sound hopeful.

Back at the office, Libby Doneger looked up from the switchboard and smiled herself into concentric circles. Hank grinned back, said, "Morning, Libby. Any messages?"

"Mr. Ronald Drury called," she said. "He must be the one in the Vivian Vixen case. Hank, tell me."

"Tell you what?"

"Tell me about it. About Vivian Vixen. Did you really know her?"

Somebody's incoming call saved Hank and he picked up the slip with the message and walked into his office. His mail contained some odds and ends of business that would amount to ten dollars or so, some advertising offers which, if accepted, would put him in hock for three years, and a civil-service announcement. The exam for probation officer would be given in October, and application forms could be obtained at city hall. Hank picked up his phone and called Drury.

The mild, gentle voice sounded tired. "Oh, Hank, I called you before, I'd like to see you."

"Fine, but better stay away from my office. Like me to come to your place?"

"Oh, no, not here. Suppose I drive past your building and pick you up. I can start now and be there in about fifteen minutes."

"Good. I'll be waiting."

When Hank stepped into the car a quarter of an hour later, he saw that Drury's face was drawn and sad, with a network of threadlike lines crisscrossing the usually smooth skin. He held out a limp little hand and said, "It's been awful, Hank. I hardly slept last night."

"I'm sorry. I know it's been tough on you."

Drury merely sighed, and concentrated on traffic. He drove slowly and cautiously, and he left the business district as soon as he could. He parked on a shady, residential street and switched off the motor. The air-conditioner hummed comfortably.

"Hank," he began, speaking in a monotone, as if any sudden inflection of his voice would bring on the headache that had just eased off. "I owe you a lot. Without you to alibi me, I'd have been in an embarrassing situation. But if you'd

77

like to tell the truth, go ahead. I know how honest you are, so it's up to you."

Hank shook his head. "The story helps me, too. Let's stick with it."

Drury smiled gratefully. Then his small hands tightened on the steering wheel and his lips bulged forward, nudged by some internal pressure. "Hank," he burst out, forgetting to nurse his headache, "have you any idea who did it? Who killed her, that is?"

Hank shook his head. "How would I know?"

"It's your business, you're an investigator. I'd like to hire you to find out."

Hank laughed. "Wait a minute. What gives you the cockeyed notion that I can learn anything? You haven't been reading books about the mighty private eye, have you?"

Drury smiled gently. "No. Normally I think the police can do a far better job."

"Normally?" said Hank. "What's on your mind, Ron? I've got one chance in a thousand of getting hold of something the cops pass up, and you know it."

"That isn't true Hank, you have a sure thing. Me."

"I don't exactly understand," Hank said quietly.

"It's simple. You know I have a false alibi, so prove I killed her."

Hank turned cold inside. "Is this a confession?"

"Of course not," Drury said, smiling wanly. "I don't want you to go to the police. I want you to build up a case, and then tell Mrs. Drury what you've found out."

"Sounds crazy."

"You can do it, Hank, and I'll help all I can, like introducing you to Dick Marlin and his group. They'll tell you things they wouldn't dare mention to the police."

"But what's the point of all this?"

"I'll try to explain." Drury pursed his lips and contemplated the quiet, leafy expanse of the tree under which the car was parked. "My wife is a good person, but she's rather aggressive. While my daughter was growing up, I always gave in to Mrs. Drury. Peace and a good, secure home environment seemed more important than my own needs, and I developed a philosophy that concentrated on the inner, spiritual life. But my daughter's grown up now, she's married and she lives in California, and I've had time to think about myself. I realized how completely Mrs. Drury dominated me, and that I couldn't cope with her. Until I found someone else, I was extremely unhappy."

He reached out and touched Hank's sleeve, as if in some sort of plea. Hank said, "I don't see how—"

Drury interrupted "I hate to bother you with my troubles, but you have to understand what she—" Hank was aware of Drury's peculiar habit of never referring to Vivian by name—"what she meant to me."

"I know you were fond of each other."

"Yes. But I'm trying to say that my friendship with her changed my home life, too. Mrs. Drury had a rival and she couldn't take me for granted any more. She consulted me about dinner company and stopped inviting the people I didn't like. My domestic life became tolerable again. But now that *she's* dead, I'm right back where I was."

Hank tapped his fingers on his knee and thought of the day in his office when Mrs. Drury had revealed her hatred of Vivian and her determination to break up the affair.

"Yes?" Hank said, prompting.

"I've not only lost a close and valued friend, but my domestic peace. Mrs. Drury has no one to be jealous of, she's no longer afraid of losing me and—well, to be perfectly frank, she's walking all over me again."

"Seems to me you ought to go and get yourself another woman."

"Me?" said Drury, aghast. "If I only could! But I'd never find anyone so sympathetic. We liked being together, we had the same tastes—music, books, everything. And she needed me, Hank. No one else will ever need me that much."

"I know. You did a lot for her."

"Do you understand now? If you can prove to Mrs. Drury that I might have killed *her*, it will change everything."

"Then why not drop a few hints, and let Mrs. Drury draw her own conclusions?"

"She'd think I was asking for help."

Hank surveyed the mild little man. A killer? And yet, to his wife he'd been a dashing lover with a famous actress for his mistress. So why wouldn't Edith Drury think of him as dangerous, when aroused? A lion in sheep's clothing.

"There's just one hitch," Hank said. "A cop by the name of Mitch Taylor ran into something that made him suspect my report. Until I get him off my neck, I can't go near this case."

"The Commissioner's a friend of mine," Drury said. "I'll speak to him and see what he can do. Taylor, did you say?"

"Mitch Taylor, patrolman in the Fourteenth Precinct. He's been investigating on his own and misusing his authority."

"I'll do what I can," Drury said. "And as to the amount— will a thousand do you?" Hank nodded, and Drury said, "I'll send it to your office this afternoon, in cash, because Mrs. Drury usually goes over my canceled checks and I certainly don't want her to know what this is all about."

"Right," said Hank. "Now the best way to handle this, once I get some evidence, is to go to Mrs. Drury as if I was trying blackmail, and then bow out and leave her with her suspicions."

Drury nodded. "Yes, that's a good idea."

"Okay," Hank said. "Now let's see what we can figure out. I saw you drive out of the apartment garage around noon, but where were you in the morning?"

"Home. I had breakfast about ten-thirty, the maid served it, and then I read the paper for a while. Around eleven-fifteen, eleven-thirty at the latest, I went into my study and called my daughter in California. We spoke for ten or fifteen minutes, there'd be a record of the call."

"That takes you up to noon, after which I followed you to the Poseidon, where you had lunch."

80

Drury's face lit up. "Where you *think* I had lunch. You didn't see me eating, did you? So why couldn't I have slipped out the side door, killed her and sneaked back? Fifteen or twenty minutes is all it would take."

"Look, Ron. Nobody commits a murder between the second and third course, and then comes back and finishes lunch."

Drury sighed. "I suppose not. But it would be all the more impressive, wouldn't it? Just think of the cold-bloodedness of it."

Hank gazed at Drury's small, intent face. He was like a child playing a game. Maybe, after Hank had talked a while, he could get into the spirit of the game and play it without feeling silly.

"It's about the only time you could have done it," Hank remarked. "Officially, I had you in sight all the way up to Raffneyville. And as a matter of fact, I did start to follow you when you left the restaurant. But after a few blocks, I gave up."

"You didn't believe me?" Ron said, shocked.

Hank, disregarding the accusation in Drury's voice, continued to think aloud. "Even if you'd turned back, you couldn't have gone all the way across town and back, and then reached Raffneyville by four-fifteen. Impossible. So let's say you never had lunch, that you simply walked into the restaurant and straight out the back, and so you fooled me."

"That's a wonderful idea."

"Except for the waiter. He'd probably remember you."

"Myron served me, he always does, but he'd do anything I asked him to. I could tell him to deny seeing me."

"Do that," Hank said gruffly. "But warn him to tell the truth to the police, if they ask." He fixed Drury with a stare and could almost feel the little man wriggle. "Now let's get to the check you gave Miss Vixen last week. She didn't need money, she had a good income, and yet you went ahead and forked out three thousand. Why?"

81

"To make Mrs. Drury jealous." Ron swallowed in embarrassment. "That's why I gave it by check, so that Mrs. Drury would see the entry when she balanced the checkbook at the end of the month."

"She'd be scared to death of you, if she found *that* out," Hank said.

Drury sighed helplessly, and Hank glowered. He was trying to build up his sense of reality, he told himself. And it was tough going.

"What did Miss Vixen do with the money?" he asked.

"I told you. She cashed it and made a down payment on that estate in Raffneyville."

"Do you know that for a fact, or is that what she said?"

Drury nodded quickly. "She said so, on Saturday. I hadn't thought of it's not being true."

"I'll look into it."

"Yes, do. I can phone Dick Marlin, he's at Raffneyville now. I'll tell him you're a friend of mine and you'd like to go up there for a day or two and ask some questions. That way, you'll have plenty of time. I'm sure you can make him talk."

"What about?"

"Well," Drury said, "there's his failure to meet me on Sunday. I went to the house first and waited for him and then, because I like to hear the local gossip, I went to the village and phoned him from there."

"Did he explain why he'd stayed in town?"

"No, not really. He kept saying he'd spoken to Vivian at noon and she'd been upset and trying to reach me."

"What was she upset about?"

"He didn't know, and there was no answer when I called her, so I decided to see her first thing Monday morning. I was on my way in—not too early, of course. I didn't want to hit that Monday morning traffic. I was on my way in when I heard the news item on the radio."

"Yes?"

"It was a shock. I pulled over to the side of the road, and I sat there. I must have looked pretty shaken up, because a

82

state trooper saw me and stopped to ask what the matter was. When I told him, he phoned in and found out they wanted me. I had a police escort the rest of the way. I wish Mrs. Drury could have seen that."

"What it comes down to," said Hank, "is that you want the details of that call of Marlin's. What makes you think he'll tell me?"

Drury looked unhappy. "I don't know. But he owes me money, I have some mortgages on his properties. You might threaten him with their foreclosure."

"Let's get back to Miss Vixen," Hank said. "You saw her Saturday night. What did you talk about?"

"Business, for a while, and then we read some passages from a book. After that—well—" Little Drury looked dreamy.

"*The Chronicle* says she had a date on Sunday."

"I read the account. The police said she'd been lying on the couch and doing her nails, and she'd had a drink. The gown she was going to wear was one of those daring creations that—but I guess you read about it. It was spread out on her bed, and she had a brand new bottle of perfume. I'd given it to her on Saturday night."

"And she was using it for some other guy."

"Hank, I know she had lovers, she'd always had them and I didn't mind." The fan of wrinkles that spread across Drury's forehead was like the contour pattern of miniature plowing. "We often discussed them, I was quite friendly with one or two of them."

"Any idea whom she had that date with?"

Drury nodded, and Hank felt a pulse beat at his throat. Give him the name of whoever Vivian had been waiting for, and it was either the murderer or one step away from him. Hank could go to the police, and his troubles would be over, the false report would be irrelevant. He'd lose a thousand-dollar fee, but it would be worth it.

"Of course I know who it was," Drury said. "She told me. In fact, I helped make the arrangements."

83

"Well?" Hank said. "Who?"

Drury shrank back into the corner of the seat. "You," he said shakily. "You."

7

THE TRAFFIC WAS light, and an hour and a quarter after Hank had started, he made the Raffneyville turn and passed the general store which was the heart of the village. A little beyond, he took a narrow, winding road that dropped off to the right. He followed it around a couple of sharp curves and reached a pair of monumental, concrete posts. They were badly cracked, and they supported rusty, wrought iron gates that hadn't been closed in years. The name, Marlin, barely decipherable, was scrawled on a plank that was propped against one of the posts.

Usually Hank turned around at this point, with his job done and Drury bedded up for the night. Except on that one occasion when he'd gone to the house and met Celia.

Thinking of her and hoping she'd remember him, Hank squeezed past the gate and drove a hundred yards or so through woods. He emerged in an open, parklike area, with broad meadows broken up by clumps of trees and bushes. The house, an Elizabethan mansion with great, cracked beams imbedded in stucco, loomed imposingly.

Hank stopped in front of the arched doorway, climbed out and hauled his bag from the trunk. The door of the house creaked, swung open, and a girl with honey-colored bangs stepped out. She was wearing shorts and holding a tiny, flowered parasol with lace on the edges.

She halted abruptly. "Oh!" she exclaimed.

Hank froze and his dark eyes dug at her. He remembered

84

her the way she'd looked last Sunday, with her thick make-up and her luscious, crimson mouth, and the flow of her body like syrup under her thin, yellow dress.

There was no dress now. Just handkerchief shorts, and a strip of cloth over her breasts. The rest of her was sleek golden skin.

"Who are you?" he asked slowly.

She stepped back, as if her seminakedness put her at a disadvantage. "I'm all confused," she said. "Dick said some-one was coming, a friend of Ron's, he didn't mention your name."

"Hank Greenleaf," he said. "You know that. And you?"

"I'm your hostess, Liz Browne." Her voice purred and she managed to smile, but she was still tense. Her knuckles were white from clutching the ridiculous little parasol. "Come in," she added. "Won't you?"

"Thanks," Hank said, and walked past her into the dark-ness of a large foyer. He blinked, and in the dimness he noticed the portrait of a woman, so sharply distorted that he wasn't quite certain.

"Vivian?" he asked, pointing.

"Yes. She had a mania for being painted, from old photo-graphs. I did that one. Do you like it?"

"Sure. You're an artist?"

Liz Browne practically melted away in her own smile. "Why, that's the nicest thing you could possibly have said."

"You bring out the better side of me," Hank said drily. He dropped his bag with a thump. "Except when you walk in on me in a strange house."

"It was awful," she said, with a shudder. "I keep thinking about it. Because all the time we were talking, she must have been lying in the next room. And you knew it."

"I didn't want you to see."

"Let's not talk about it." Liz fidgeted with her parasol. "I'll show you your room, shall I?" She led the way up a broad stairway with carved, oak banisters. Hank picked up his bag and followed.

85

On the second floor, she went down a wide corridor and entered a spacious room containing a bed and an upholstered chair and a fancy chaise longue, and not much else. He dropped his bag carelessly on the chair, and a thin cloud of dust floated up. He sneezed, thinking that Liz was a hell of a housekeeper.

"The house is for sale," she said. "That's why it's only half-furnished. Dick opened it for the summer, but he won't spend money on it. He expected Vivian to buy it."

"And what happens now?"

"I guess we're stuck with it. If the bareness bothers you, you can always look at the view. It's lovely, I look at it all day long."

Hank stepped to the window and gazed at the panorama of valley spread out below. It was farm country, with the fields squared off in a variety of fresh, salad colors. Miniature houses and barns dotted the landscape.

Hank turned his back to the window and swept Liz with frank, unabashed interest. "Nice to look at," he remarked.

"Why don't you put on a bathing suit?" she said quickly, twirling the parasol. "The pool's in back, Dick's there and so is Ben. There are just the three of us."

"Ben?" said Hank.

"My brother. I thought you knew who everybody was."

"No. Ron didn't say anything. Would you mind straightening me out? You say you're my hostess. Do you live here?"

"Oh, no. Ben and I work for Dick Marlin. Ben's his accountant, and I help sell, but the office is closed for a few days and we came out here to rest. We're like a family, the three of us. Ever since my parents died, a long time ago, Dick's been like a father. He gave me a job and helped put Ben through school and he's just wonderful. You'll love him."

"And Vivian? Where did she fit in?"

"Dick sold her a house when she came to town, and after that we became friends and he invested for her. She had her own room here and she came out weekends."

"With Ron?"

86

"Yes, he'd bring her." Liz glanced around the room. "If there's anything you need, just tell me. Your towels are on the rack, and the bathroom's next door." Her low voice, purring pleasantly, rose in ecstasy. "Isn't it a *heavenly* day?"

"What were you doing at headquarters?" Hank asked. "Why did the police question you?"

Liz climbed down from her heights. "Because I knew her," she said sharply. "Because she did business with us. Now tell me what *you* were doing at headquarters."

"Went to see you," Hank said.

"And walked past me as if I were poison." Her large, pale eyes rested on Hank. "I went to that bar last night," she said abruptly. "But there was someone with you, so I left."

"I know. I couldn't shake him, and I didn't want him to see you."

"Who was he?"

"A cop."

"Oh." She absorbed the information with feelings unfathomable to Hank. "I'll see you at the pool," she said serenely.

He watched her walk out, flat-footed and graceful, like a ballet dancer. Then he got the towel, slung it over his shoulder and went next door to the bathroom. After he'd washed, he put on his black, bathing trunks and went downstairs, past Liz's portrait of Vivian. Through a doorway, he saw the oak-paneling of a large, imposing room. Curious, he stepped inside.

Except for a few wicker chairs and a card table, the room was bare, but a portrait of Vivian above the fieldstone fireplace gave warmth and substance. Hank studied it, then crossed the room to a door at the far end. He had his hand on the knob when Celia's voice stopped him.

"Oh, Mr. Greenleaf. *You*—you're Mr. Greenleaf?"

He turned around and saw Celia's round, fat, beaming face. "Yes," he said. "So you remember me."

"Course I do. But Mr. Greenleaf, please. That door's locked. Nobody goes in there."

"Why not?"

"It was Miss Vivian's room." The dark, round face grew solemn and worried. "The police here, they closed it, they asked me to tell if anybody goes in. And I don't want nobody to go there and touch her things. 'Tain't decent."

"I'm sorry," Hank said. "I was trying to find the pool, and I guess I got lost."

Celia's voice softened. "The pool? It's in back, you go past the stairs and straight out. And Mr. Greenleaf, anything you want to make yourself comfortable, you just ask me."

"Thanks," Hank said. "Feed me plenty, and I'll love you."

Celia was all grin. Hank said, "By the way, who was here when Mr. Drury came on Sunday?"

"Just me. He expected Mr. Marlin, there was some kind of mix-up, and Mr. Marlin hadn't come up, or phoned, either. Mr. Drury, he was real upset, he said he'd had a long, slow trip with all that traffic, and he could have stayed home."

"What time was that?"

Celia burst out laughing. "Lord love you!" she said. "You followed him, you know what time it was. 'Bout quarter-past four."

"That's right," Hank said. "Then what?"

"He sat around kind of restless, and after a while he went down to the village, for company. Visited the mayor and gave him a big check for the fire department."

"And no else was here?"

"Nobody except me, so in the evening we talked some, mostly about Miss Vivian. Mr. Greenleaf, you been reading all that stuff in the papers, how she give big parties and everybody get drunk and do things?"

"Sure. How could anybody miss it?"

"It ain't true. She was decent, she was real decent. Maybe she was a little free with her loving, but that's what God give us a body for. And the truth is she was lonesome, and she couldn't never forget that awful accident that happened to her. It was a terrible thing, and I expect Mr. Drury, he was the only man in the world really loved her, without wanting anything from her."

88

"What did the others want?"

"Ain't for me to say." She pivoted slowly, like a liner circling to head into the channel. Then, gazing at Hank with dark, brooding eyes, she added crisply, "Money." And she waddled off toward the kitchen.

Outside the house, Hank saw a wide terrace, broken by a flight of broad steps descending to the pool. It was a good hundred feet long, painted blue inside and white along the lip. A couple of striped umbrella-tables gave the scene a smart, stylish, summer-resort look.

Liz Browne was lying on the grass, and she was asleep. Her gay little parasol was upended, with the handle stuck in the ground. The spread was big enough to shade her face.

No one else was in sight, and Hank went down the steps, treading gingerly on the hot stones. At the bottom, he jumped onto the cool grass, landed on a pebble and said, "Ouch!"

Liz awoke. She turned her head and saw Hank.

"Hello," she called lazily. "You took so long, I must have fallen asleep."

He came over to her, circled the parasol and dropped to his knees. "Where's everybody?" he asked.

She looked around in surprise. "I don't know. There's just you and me, all alone in the world."

"And Celia," he said.

Liz nodded. "Celia, of course." She gave Hank a lovelorn sigh and said, "We need Celia to cook, don't we?"

"I don't know. I can cook pretty good."

"Oh, Hank!" she said, still playing with him. "You're so wonderful."

He squinted in the sun and stared down at her. He could see the gleaming dots of perspiration on her soft, polished skin. Her breasts, barely covered, rolled languidly as she flexed her arms. Her lips parted in a faint, drowsy smiling, and their undersides were pink and wet.

"You and me," Hank said, "and nothing to bother us. This is quite a place."

"I love luxury."

"I know. You go for orchids, don't you?"

Liz rolled to her side and sat up, raising her knees, clasping her hands across them and using her knuckles for a chinrest. Her anxious face seemed to shine through the heavy veneer of make-up.

"I thought we weren't going to talk about that," she said.

"You're wrong. I'd like to straighten out exactly what happened on Sunday. You see, I heard you moving around in front of the door for a couple of minutes, before you came in. You had quite a time making up your mind to risk it."

"You must have been nervous, waiting and not knowing who was out there."

"Sure I was nervous," he said. "Tell me, what did you do with the orchids?"

"I took them home. Why?"

"They were wrapped in a ribbon, with the name of the florist on it."

"I didn't notice. The flowers weren't fresh. They wilted in the heat and I had to throw them out."

"Remember the ribbon?"

She unclasped her hands and lowered them, and she spoke as if she were out of breath. "No. I don't remember the ribbon." Then looking past him, she brightened up. "Oh, there they are now." She raised her voice, and she waved. "Ben, Dick—where were you? Mr. Greenleaf is here, come and meet him."

Hank watched the two men approach. The younger one wore bathing trunks. He was dark, like Hank, and about Hank's build, but he had strong, even features. That was Ben, Hank supposed. Which meant that the little guy with the Roosevelt chin must be Marlin. He had on blue slacks and a fancy sport-shirt, and he trotted over energetically and pumped Hank's hand with enthusiasm.

"Hello, Hank, glad to meet you. My profound and desolate apologies for being in absentia when you arrived. But Ben and I paid a call at the springhouse to persuade the presiding deity to try a little harder. You see, lots of water, no worries; dry spell, and I'm personally responsible. I sold a beauty of a place up in the Laurel Hill section a couple of years ago, and the well went back on my promise and I ended up in court. Had to swear in every rain-drop and put it on the stand and hope it didn't evaporate on cross-examination. Liz, make us some drinks, like a good girl." Marlin rattled on nervously. "She's the best bartender you ever saw. Turns gin into nectar and whisky into wassail. Been swimming, Hank?"

Hank stood up lazily. "Not yet, but I think I'll have a quick one, and then relax."

After his dip, he lounged under the umbrella and sipped one of Liz's masterpieces. Ben, dark and virile, with a towel draped over his shoulders and with the air of an athlete who'd just won his heat, gulped one and dawdled over his second. Marlin rubbed the stem of his glass, while his talk erupted in hyperbolic flashes. Liz kept glancing at Hank with adoration in her eyes.

Hank sensed that the trio were waiting for the right moment to jump. They must have worked together on so many deals that they had no need to plan or rehearse. They played Hank by ear, so to speak. When he hinted at Drury's possible guilt, Marlin vibrated with praise of him and Liz made it clear that she regarded him as one step above St. Francis of Assisi, if only because Ron was wealthier.

The subject of the three-thousand dollars, however, was something else again. It made Ben angry, Liz sullen and Marlin voluble. He said Vivian hadn't given him the money, he'd never seen it. And it was no secret that he needed it badly. He had funds tied up in this house, it was a white elephant, and he'd been counting on Vivian to take it off his hands. That was why he'd called her on Sunday. Twice. He'd been anxious to close the deal, he couldn't face Ron until Vivian had made her deposit, and in cash.

Marlin told how she must have been lying there dead, while he had bad thoughts about her for not answering the phone. As he expounded on the scene, he throbbed with emotion and his voice quivered. His dear, dear friend whom life had treated so cruelly, and whose lot he had tried to ameliorate by making her dollars grow.

He leaned forward, tapped Hank's knee and grew confidential. Understand this: Vivian was careless about money, the three-thousand might be tucked away in the corner of a drawer or stuffed in one of her pocketbooks. Or maybe a cop had found it. A cop with sticky fingers. How about that?

Hank was more than willing to think about that. A cop who'd been kicked off the Homicide Squad—he'd have sticky fingers. But the fantasy that Taylor had stolen three-thousand dollars comforted Hank only momentarily. It was a long ways between *might have* and *did*.

"You said you called her twice," Hank remarked. "What about the first time?"

Marlin's teeth glistened whitely in a smile that gave all. "I didn't mention it to the police," he said, "and I'm sure you won't, either. No point to it."

Hank tried to digest the remark. Until now, he felt that he was being had. Marlin whipped up a tangle of words, he snarled the meanings hopelessly. He was like a magician performing his act, but instead of pulling a rabbit out of his hat, he produced a mess of stale *hazenpfeffer*. And the smell was not good.

"What did she say?" Hank asked.

"I can't quote her verbatim," Marlin said. "And if I could, I certainly wouldn't repeat her language in front of Liz. But I imagine the phone company had to reinsulate the wires, they weren't made for quite so much heat."

"She said?" Hank asked, coaxing.

"That if she didn't get hold of Ron soon, she'd commit murder, mayhem and malediction, she'd blow the roof off her house and wipe out real estate values in the whole north end of town."

"Why was she so mad at Ron?"

"She wasn't angry at *him*. She wanted him for comfort,

balm and assuagement. She needed his healing spirit and his mellifluous words."

"Is that why she was drinking and fixing her nails, and had that dress spread out on her bed?"

"Why, Hank," Marlin said, beaming with good will. "You can answer that better than I can. A big, powerful guy like you."

"Meaning what?"

Liz answered. "Dick knows you were there."

"And that you were too," Hank said to her. "Involve me, and you involve yourself." Liz looked startled, and Ben glowered. "I think I'll have another swim," Hank added. "Anyone coming?"

He stood up, crossed the grass to the pool and dived in. The water slid coolly along his body, and the feel was clean and refreshing. He swam with an easy, rhythmic stroke, and his mind worked with precision.

It struck him that he'd been sent here not to gather evidence against Ron, but against one of these three. Ron himself lacked the force and the aggression to pound down. He'd decided to expose Hank to the Marlin group in the hope that they'd give themselves away.

And they were doing it. By their defensiveness. Marlin with his talk of financial trouble, Liz with her amorous flirting. And Hank felt certain that there was more to come.

Turning at the end of a lap, he saw Ben step to the tip of the springboard, pose and then flip himself up and out. He cut the water with hardly a splash.

Hank churned the length of the pool, rolled onto his back and floated idly. When he noticed Ben sitting on the edge of the pool, Hank swam over, hauled himself up and wiped his eyes.

"Feels good," he said. He pushed his shoulders back and inflated his chest.

Ben, with his feet dangling in the water, kicked idly. "Hank," he said, "I just met you. We don't know each other, but sometimes things have to happen fast. So I'm going to be direct."

"Sure. Why not?"

"What you said before about not involving yourself without involving Liz—don't count on it. Suppose the police got an anonymous call, asking them to look for a piece of cloth caught on a certain rose bush, and then to match it up with your pants. That wouldn't bring Liz in, would it?"

Hank stared at Ben's strong, tanned body encased in the fancy bright-colored trunks. "No." Hank said, "But I think it would bring you in. Because you must have been the one that opened the door, and run away when I yelled."

"Liz and I were together all afternoon," Ben said. "And ready to swear to it."

Ben smiled smugly, and Hank, studying him, decided Ben was the the weak link. Marlin hid behind his verbal fireworks, and Liz behind her sex-appeal. But Ben seethed with hostility, he was bursting with suppressions, and he was overconfident. Lead him on, and he'd probably say more than he should.

"Forget it," Hank said. "You don't have to worry about me." He yawned lazily. "What struck me was, when Liz and Dick were defending Ron and explaining how wonderful he is, you didn't say a word."

"Everybody loves him. Do I have to join the parade, too?" Ben pursed his lips and looked bothered.

"I'm not one of his admirers, either," Hank said, watching Ben narrowly. "Tell me why you don't like him."

"I just don't believe in him," Ben burst out. "Nobody's that selfless unless he's trying to sell a bill of goods. When Dick unloaded a real turkey on him, for instance, what did Ron do? He thanked Dick for getting him a tax cut. Ron and his moneybags."

"He knows the real estate business pretty thoroughly, doesn't he?"

"You bet he does, and nobody can put anything over on him. He let Dick think he was being slick, but—"

"But what?"

"Nothing, except that it's all an act. Like the way he followed Vivian around with those moon eyes of his—let me tell you something, Hank. She was his girl friend, wasn't she?"

"Everybody knows that."

"All right. One night I'm here in the pool and we have no clothes on and we're not just swimming, either, and Ron comes down and sees us. He says, 'Excuse me,' and goes back, and the next morning he takes me aside and tells me not to worry, he isn't jealous. Is that natural?"

"I guess he accepted her the way she was," Hank remarked. "He knew she was no angel."

Ben's feet ruffled the water. "Meaning those parties?"

"What about them? What were they?"

"Movies," Ben said in a low, confidential tone. "Fifty bucks admission, and you know the kind they were."

"She could have gotten into real trouble for that."

"She paid off the police. I was there when one of them happened to come around."

Hank slapped his thigh. Vivian lived in the Fourteenth precinct, Taylor worked there. Graft? Or something far worse?

Hank said excitedly, "That cop—what was his name?"

"How do I know? He was at the door when I came one day, and she had a hundred bucks for him."

"What did he look like? Stocky, medium height? Brown eyes, and hair brushed back?"

"I guess so, but I didn't notice particularly. What's the difference?"

"A strut to him, and a habit of rolling his shoulders? High-pitched voice?"

"That's right, but what of it?"

"*He* might have killed her. A crooked cop, and you saw the pay off! Ben, we've got him cold."

"Don't get so worked up," Ben said. "What I'm telling you is confidential, and I didn't actually see the pay off. Although it might be easy to show, if you knew his name."

95

"I know his name all right. How do you show it?"

"She kept an account-book with a list of every payment she made. I did her tax work, and she used to be so careless that I told her to put everything down. After that, I never saw anybody so methodical. And those hick cops—" Ben shook his head, as if he couldn't quite believe.

"What about them?" Hank asked.

"They must have had hold of that book. I can just see them." Ben spoke through his nose and performed his imitation with seasoned expertness. "Rube says to Hiram, 'Hi, you figure we ought to check her addition?' And Hiram thinks it over real careful and says to Rube, 'Rube, you know dang well I never did learn much arithmetic'." Ben leaned back and rocked with laughter. When he had finished appreciating himself he said, "What a picnic for a blackmailer!"

Hank gave Ben a grin calculated to satisfy Ben's ego. Then Hank got back to the subject that interested him. "You mean the book is up here?"

"That's where she usually kept it." Ben leaned back on his elbows and craned his neck in the direction of the house. "You can almost see her room from here," he said bitterly. "Locked, with the windows nailed up. And Celia guarding it as if the royal jewels were inside."

"You sound as if you'd like to get in," Hank observed.

"Who wouldn't? And there's nothing to it, once Celia leaves."

"She's going?" Hank asked in surprise.

"Tomorrow's her day off. She usually leaves the night before, as soon as the dishes are washed, and then she walks to the gate where somebody picks her up. So how about looking tomorrow?"

"Sure, but why invite me? What for?"

"Because if I did it alone, Liz might find out and she'd get mad at me, she'd call it stealing or something. But if I go along with you, that's different, it's like an adventure. You take what suits your fancy, and I take what suits mine." Ben held held out his hand. "Partners, Hank? Partners?"

Hank did not shake hands. A guy who threatened one minute and made a complete about-face the next—Hank wanted none of it. He wondered why Ben was letting him in on the venture, and decided that Ben was scared to go alone. So Hank shrugged, intending to pass the incident off lightly. But Ben snapped angrily.

"What's the matter? Don't you trust me?"

"Skip it," Hank said. "Nothing to get upset about."

Ben scowled, started to swear and then cut himself off. "Liz," he said in a low voice. "She's coming."

Hank turned. Liz, carrying two cocktail glasses, was walking along the edge of the pool. She must have noticed the scene between Hank and Ben, but her voice, floating lazily through the hot, heavy air, gave no indication of it. Instead, her words were tactful.

"If the boys won't come to the bar," she said, "then the bar comes to them."

"Good-looking bar," Hank remarked.

"Who asked you?" Ben demanded irritably.

The slight lift of Liz's eyebrows told Hank that she was provoked by Ben's remark, but she said nothing. However, she proceeded to show her feelings by giving Hank all her attention, and Ben none.

She halted next to Hank, with her bare thigh brushing his shoulder. He was conscious of the warm, pleasant odor of her body, an odor of flesh and perspiration combined with the perfume of the sun lotion she'd been using. Her smile was frankly flirtatious as she leaned down and handed him a glass.

Hank was aware of Ben's increasing annoyance. Ben started to say something, changed his mind. He reached down and flipped a handful of water in her face.

She jerked back, spilling most of her drink. "Oh, Ben!" she exclaimed. "You got me all wet."

He grinned impishly. "Sorry," he said, and he bent forward and kissed her feet.

With his apology, she restored him to her good graces and

97

cut Hank off completely. Her smile was all for Ben as she said coquettishly, "You silly, you!" Ben gazed up with adoration, and her fatuous glance melted over him.

Hank was bothered by the over-closeness of brother and sister, and suddenly he wished Jean was here, sitting next to him and stirring the water with her big toe. Jean, familiar and reliable and devoted to him. Bright-eyed, and sniffing with her too-long nose. Filled with thoughts of Toby and love and domesticity, and sex every Saturday night.

Liz's voice broke in, as if from a distance. "What were you boys talking about?"

"Nothing," Ben said quickly. "A private matter. Nothing that concerns you."

Liz rumpled Ben's hair and gave him a tender look. "Dope," she said lightly. "I don't believe you. You were probably telling Hank how you dislike Ron and won't trust him."

"And if I was?" Ben demanded. "I'm entitled to my own opinion of him."

"Of course you are, but it bothers me when you say nasty things. Particularly about Ron, who never did you any harm." She turned to Hank, and her eyes lit up and she spoke earnestly. "Ron is sweet," she said, "and I wish there were more people like him. He's always doing favors, he likes everybody. And he was generosity itself to Vivian. Not just money, but understanding and sympathy, all the things that count. It was just wonderful to see them together."

"Don't defend him so passionately," Ben remarked. "Hank will think you're in love."

Hank turned away. A brother and sister arguing, not quite amiably. Their parents had died long ago and she'd supported Ben and taken care of him and put him through school, and she was tied to him. Obviously she was strong and he was weak, but they worked in the same office and she reacted to his moods and squandered all her affection on him.

Well, let her. If she had psychological problems, Hank

98

wanted none of them. With a grimace, he lifted his glass, gulped the contents and stood up. He balanced himself on the edge of the pool and dived in. He touched the concrete bottom with the tips of his fingers and pushed up. He shot to the surface like a cork.

Ben was crossing the grass and heading for the table with the striped umbrella, but Liz waited. She kept watching Hank. When he swam over and put his hands on the lip of concrete, she covered them with her foot. She pressed her toes against his fingers and rubbed gently.

"Hank," she said in a low, teasing voice. "Why did you run away from me?"

8

HANK SLEPT FITFULLY that night, and thoughts and images swirled through his mind with a strange, disordered logic. Partly, he was unsure which he had dreamed and which was real.

There were voices, there was a door closing, perhaps his, and at one time lights flashed. He was certain he heard a car, and that was the one event which was explicable. For Ben had gone to the village shortly after dinner, and the car was probably his, returning.

There were other incidents which Hank obviously dreamed. He saw Taylor, for instance, leaving Mario's bar and saying again, "I'll be seeing you, huh?" And in the dream Hank answered and said, "Naturally. Tomorrow night, for another beer."

Hank saw Vivian's record book, too, with a hand reaching for it, and the hand was Taylor's. With that, Vivian's murder came clear, with Taylor as the killer. He'd visited her on Sunday to collect his graft. He wanted more money and she refused, and there was a short, angry scene in which she castigated him and threatened to expose him and produce her records of the payments. He killed her, and he was still there when Hank rang the bell.

In the dream, Taylor ran out the back door and saw Hank enter and lie down on the couch and drink the orange juice. And so, to protect himself, Taylor fastened on Hank, because Taylor knew Hank had been there.

Hank woke without reaching full consciousness, and the strange duel between Taylor and himself became perfectly comprehensible. It was a duel between an innocent man who couldn't admit his presence at Vivian's, and a guilty man who couldn't accuse without giving himself away. They were like the guard and the prisoner who were handcuffed to each other. They ate together and slept together and traveled together, and which one was the prisoner and which the guardian was sometimes confused, for they shared a greater guilt that transcended the actual crime.

Hank's thinking about Taylor was never quite clear. The result, the relationship, the sense of loyalty to the proposition of their involvement remained with Hank, but the precise reasoning underlying it never emerged into full consciousness. He was left with the certainty of his commitment to see Taylor nightly, for both of them had transgressed, and their expiation must be mutual.

In the gray, dull light of early dawn, Hank woke fully and began thinking about Ben. A way in which he might tie Ben into the case occurred to Hank, and he decided to work on it as soon as he got back to the city. He felt a profound distrust of Ben; he had no desire to share anything with him, and least of all, Vivian's private records. So why wait, Hank asked himself, when he could go downstairs now and investigate on his own?

Hank got out of bed. He could pick a lock as well as the next man, and the lock of Vivian's room was not a complicated one. Hank found a wire hanger in his closet, he bent the end, left his room quietly and went downstairs.

Vivian's portrait over the mantel was a soft, smiling, face emerging from the dark background of paint. A face to fall in love with, as millions had.

He walked past the portrait and stooped down to examine the lock. It looked easy enough. But first, he put his hand on the knob and turned it. To his surprise, the door opened. He stepped inside.

The first thing he saw was the great, massive mound of flesh that had been Celia humped on the floor. The handle of a kitchen knife protruded from her chest, and in the dim light her blood was dark and gleaming. He approached slowly, to make sure that she was dead.

He gazed trancelike, in horror. Standing there and thinking of her great, easy kindness, he was obsessed with the cruelty and the senselessness of her murder. What could Celia have possibly done, to provoke this act? Whom had *she* ever harmed?

Hank clenched his fists hard, as if the power of his empty grip could somehow work evil on the perpetrator of the crime. He turned slowly and let his eyes slide along the chairs, the bed, the dresser, the closed door of the closet. He saw nothing that was disarranged, he found no sign of search or seeking. Then he noticed the shiny object near his feet and he stooped down and picked up a small, brown button.

He fingered it purposelessly, telling himself he ought to leave it here for the police, and then telling himself that he'd be a suspect, that he might derive some benefit by keeping this bit of evidence which was probably a clue to the murderer. Still holding the button, he turned slowly and left the room. He closed the door with careful quietness.

Outside, he stood stiffly for maybe a half-minute. He was looking at the portrait, but he saw nothing and felt nothing. Crazy, religious clichés began forming in his mind. We walk in the shadow of the valley of death. Man is mortal, and to each one, his time comes. Ashes to ashes and dust to—

Except that she was neither ashes nor dust. She was an

101

obscene horror, and he panicked. Twice, he thought. First Vivian, and now Celia. He'd discovered both bodies, and had held out on the police.

He moved automatically, as if he'd been wounded. His feet dragged and his knees bent like rubber and he began talking to himself, whispering to his legs. Carry me, thrust and hold, wobble and wamble, swim or slide, but support me.

He talked to the banister on the way up. Hold me, help me.

He numbered the steps, like a child learning to count. Upstairs, he walked on tiptoe. He breathed with difficulty and expected every door to open, and he had a moment of sheer terror when he reached his room. He was afraid it was the wrong one, or that he'd find someone waiting, ready to accuse.

Inside, he flung himself on the bed and tried to disbelieve what he'd seen. He hadn't been downstairs, he hadn't seen her, he'd never left his room. Let someone else find her, but not him. If he found her, he'd be questioned. Why had he gone there? Why had he come to Raffneyville? What had Ben told him about Vivian's closet?

Liz, Ben, Dick, himself. And a car in the night.

He'd know by morning.

When Hank came downstairs, Ben and Marlin were sitting at the small, folding breakfast-table. Liz, in the kitchen, was humming happily.

"Sleep well?" Dick Marlin asked.

"Fine. Beautiful day for the country, isn't it?"

Dick grinned. "The gods blow hot and cold, Hank. They give with one hand and take away with the other, and they put dollar signs in the azure sky. I have to go to town on business."

Hank frowned. Last night Marlin had said something about a picnic, if the weather was nice. And with no mail delivery here and no phone ring that Hank had heard, how could Marlin suddenly have business?

Ben answered the unspoken question. "Client of ours that I saw in the village last night. The three of us have to get to work, so I guess our little project is off, too."

"Must be quite a place you went to," Hank said sarcastically. "You meet everybody worthwhile, don't you?"

Ben seemed surprised at the attack. "What makes you say that?" He turned to Dick and said, "He wasn't here was he? You said you didn't see him."

"Who?" Hank demanded

"That cop we were talking about," Ben said. "He came into the bar last night and asked how to get here."

"You saw Taylor?" Hank said, stunned.

"Sure. Around ten o'clock. He wanted directions. Did you see him?"

"Me? No." Hank's mind spun and he wanted to shout out the news. Taylor here, during the night. Hank let his eyes rest on the door, and he shivered. "I guess he lost his way."

"Funny his coming here," Ben said. "What for?"

"Probably wanted to see me," Hank said, still dazed. "I left word at my office where I'd be, he must have come all the way up here."

"Don't sound so important," Ben said.

Hank stood up. He went the long way around the room to reach the kitchen. There, Liz turned from the stove and said, "Good morning, Hank. Did you—" She broke off and studied him. "Hank, you look so strange."

"So do you," he said, stiffly. "You look different. Did something happen?"

"Yes, I fell in love with you," she said, smiling, teasing him. "Passionately, to distraction. Beyond all sense."

"Me, too," Hank said, "Want me to bring the coffee in?" And he reached out to take the coffeepot.

Liz handed it to him. "Hank," she said, "You've lost a button on your sleeve. Shall I sew it on for you, later?"

His heart missed a beat and he raised his arm slowly. One

103

of the two buttons on his cuff was gone, and the remaining one was the mate of the button he'd found last night, next to Celia's body.

"Well, what's the matter now?" Liz asked.

Hank managed a grin. "Nothing. I was just wondering when I could have lost it. And how you could match it up, when it's gone."

"Why, I never thought of that!" Liz said.

Hank took the coffeepot.

He had no recollection of when he'd last had that button on that sleeve. But he'd evidently dropped it, and someone had picked it up and set out, deliberately and methodically, to frame him. Liz? Ben? Dick Marlin? Or Taylor?

After breakfast Hank drove back to the city, alone. He drove fast, keyed up, and he was filled with anger and foreboding.

9

MITCH SWUNG THE patrol car into the precinct parking lot at a couple of minutes before four, and cut the motor. Oscar Henderson, sitting next to him, let out a sigh.

"Another day," he said, "and I'm glad this one's over. With half the boys working on the Vixen stuff, we sure cover territory."

"Yeah," said Mitch. "We ought to get paid by the mile, huh?"

Oscar muttered something, and swung open the door. He made a face as he got out. "The way my pants stick in this heat, some day I'm gonna get up and leave 'em behind."

"I'll tell the Commissioner about it," Mitch said. "Maybe he'll put us in shorts, like them Limeys in the tropics."

He picked up the day's report-sheets attached to the clip-board, and then he remembered the car was supposed to get greased and checked over, and so he should have run it into the garage. He said, "I got to put this thing in back, Oscar. Go on ahead."

He watched Oscar plod across the hot pavement and go in a side door of the station house. Mitch turned the starter-switch, but the engine didn't catch. Vapor lock, he supposed. He figured he'd let the mechanic handle that one, so he got out of the car to follow Oscar. Halfway across the lot he stopped, turned around and yelled at the garage entrance.

"Hey, Joe!" he called out. He saw a figure in coveralls and he said, "Number Seven-Four—I just remembered she ought to be inside. Take her, huh?" He headed for the side door without waiting for an answer.

The big barn-like room inside was cool enough, and he walked up to the desk. The sergeant said, "Lieutenant wants you, Taylor. In his office."

Mitch nodded. "He in trouble again?"

"Sure," the sergeant said drily. "He wants to consult his right-hand man about how to fix up this weather. They say it's going to rain tonight and get cooler."

Mitch signed his report, checked it over and handed it to the sergeant. "Cooler?" Mitch said. "Maybe it'll get down to ninety." He took his cap off and wiped his forehead. Then, with a cocky set to his shoulders, he turned and marched to the small office at the rear.

In answer to his knock, Lieutenant (Acting) Pisani's voice said, "Come in."

Mitch entered. "You wanted to see me, Lieutenant?"

Pisani was built compact, like a wad of rammed earth, and his bristly hair could have been driven onto his skull with a turret-press.

"We got a complaint about you, Taylor," the lieutenant said in a brittle voice. "From the Commissioner's office. Some civilian claims you're riding him, on the Vixen case. What's it about?"

105

"Me?" Mitch said in surprise. "Oh, it must be that private detective, lives over on Cooper Street. What's he beefing about?"

Pisani's eyes dropped to a note stuck in the corner of his desk-blotter. "Violation of Section 487-B. Unauthorized investigation, unfounded accusations. Let's hear it, Taylor."

"Nothing much. I ran into this guy in a bar, and we had a beer together. Seeing as how you once said it was important for a cop to be friendly with the people who live in this precinct, I figured I'd chew the fat with him and get his angle."

"Some fat!" Pisani said coldly. "You know the Homicide Squad has sole jurisdiction and we work under their orders, don't you?"

"Sure," Mitch said cheerfully. "But just talking to a guy? Lieutenant, maybe you can give me a little advice."

"My advice is to lay off."

"Yes sir. But the thing is, I made an appointment with him, he said he might be able to turn up certain information that could be kind of important. So you want me to call in the Homicide Squad and let them handle it? Or should I see him, and then turn it over to you? If it amounts to anything, that is."

"What information?"

"Well," Mitch said, thinking hard. He wasn't going to give out and let this shoo-fly grab the credit for maybe cracking the case, so Mitch had to think up something good. "Well," he said, and the explanation that came to him wasn't too far from the truth, at that, "the guy has ideas about who drank that glass of orange juice, but when I tried to get it out of him, he clammed up. After a little discussion—and I'll admit I gave him some tough reasons—he said he'd see me again. But wouldn't it be something if we came up with who it was?" Mitch scratched his jaw. "Homicide Squad would look kind of silly, claiming we shouldn't have done it."

The *we* business got Pisani. Cut him in and maybe he'd get to be a full lieutenant, monicker and all, instead of just

106

an acting-lieutenant. He said, "I don't gag my men, and I like to think we're all on the ball. On the other hand, I'm ordering you not to investigate without proper authority, and—" he had to take a squint at the slip of paper on his desk, on account he had trouble with the big words—"and not to make unwarranted accusations. I don't want any trouble with the Commissioner."

"Yes sir," said Mitch. "You can count on me."

"Anything you find out, you'll naturally bring here."

"Sure, Lieutenant." Mitch fingered his cap and told himself that shoo-flies, they were all alike. "There's just one thing. If this guy should come around here and try to make trouble, he'll go out on his ear, huh? What I mean is, the precinct can take care of him."

Pisani grunted, which he was good at, and Mitch turned around and went out.

Downstairs in the locker room, the day shift was washing up and changing into street clothes. They kidded around as usual, and Mitch went along with them. The first thing he always did when he was transferred to a new unit, was to let them know he was regular and didn't have any ideas about getting a promotion and stepping on somebody's toes.

So he rated pretty good in the locker room. He horsed around for a while, and then, in one of those quiets that happen, he said in his high, piping voice, "Funny thing. You know this joker, Greenleaf? Private eye, he calls himself."

"Sure. What about him?"

"Cop-hater. He's got some kind of a grudge against cops. If he shows up here, you'll know him, huh?"

"What would he show up for?" a blond cop asked.

"He went to the Commissioner, claims I got it in for him. That's what I saw the lieutenant about. The lieutenant knows what the score is, so I'm just passing the word along. Big guy, black hair. If he ever comes down this street, just turn him around, huh?"

Mitch figured that would do it. The boys knew how a civilian could smear up your record, and they were ready to gang up and help out one of their own. So Mitch let it go at that. He said, "Anybody going my way? Boy, you guys are slow!"

He got a hitch as far as Hawthorne and then he took the bus. When he got out, he decided to call Greenleaf and needle him a little, and make sure about seeing him tonight. But the girl at Greenleaf's office said he'd gone up to Raffneyville, she had the phone number up there in case anyone had to get in touch.

Mitch took the number, but the funny thing was, he felt like they'd had an appointment and here the guy was sliding out on him. So maybe Mitch ought to go up and let him know he couldn't take a powder like this. Borrow Jub's car, like Mitch often did. He even had a key. And the drive up would be nice and cool, so why not?

Mitch had a two-block walk to the brick apartment where he lived. It was still hot, but he didn't mind, his T-shirt took up the sweat and the nylon thing almost felt cool, after that uniform all day.

He found Mamie and little Joey digging sand in the playground, and he fooled around with them a little and then he went on up. Gladys Freeman was there with Amy, and Mitch got the idea right off that Amy had asked her over so she could talk about the case. On account of Gladys had a pipeline.

She looked different from the way she did in the old days. When she used to sit outside Decker's office and type his stuff, she always wore a white blouse that was kind of frilly, and she seemed cool and clean and efficient. But she was softer now, she kind of beamed out, and she wore dresses that showed what she had. Still, alongside Amy, she seemed half dead. But then, everybody did.

Mitch sat down and said something about the heat. Amy gave him a can of beer and he opened it and the cold, bubbly stuff tasted good.

Amy said, "Jub's coming later on," and Glad said, "He's been working hard, I made him promise to take time off for dinner. Because, even though he still has a lot to do, the pressure is off. I guess things can wait, now."

Mitch settled back. "How's it stacking up?" he asked.

Amy relaxed, like she'd set this up and was a little leary Mitch would be sore at her for trying to take over. But with his question she saw it was okay, and so she perked up like a kid just out of school.

Gladys pulled up a chair, and a little line cut into her fore-head, like she was trying to get her mind organized. "Bill Decker said it's the kind of case where he wished he had a hundred men, instead of eight."

"He's got the whole damn department," Mitch said. "Half the Fourteenth are working just for him."

"Yes, but you know what I mean. Trained men. He had a list of forty-three names of her intimate friends, all male, and he had to check on alibis from every single one of them. And that takes time."

"I didn't know any dame could handle forty-three guys," Mitch said.

Amy bubbled up with, "Not all at once." Mitch said, "How would you know?" Amy made a face at him, and Gladys laughed and said "That reminds me about those dresses she had. Jub calls them gasket-weave because they fit tight between her—well, you know what I mean," she added, blushing.

"Did Jub tell you about those pictures in the green album?" Mitch said. "In color, too. With stuff like that, I could be a real camera fan."

"I'm glad you didn't have the chance," Amy said. "I won-der when she wore those dresses. Whether she put them on for those parties of hers."

"Private showing," Mitch said. "Like the guy she had a date with, on Sunday. There she had that dress out on the bed, ready to put on, and she was in the middle of fixing her nails, and then something happened. And if you ask me, the guy that killed her wasn't the guy she had the date with. It was somebody else, somebody she wasn't even expecting."

Mitch made like he was thinking hard. "Big, tall guy," he said.

"Because of the angle of the knife?" Gladys said. "That's what Bill and Jub both thought, too, but somehow it seemed too logical. So I made Jub act it out with me. I pretended to run away from him and then I stumbled. Look." She held up her arm and showed a black-and-blue mark. "I hit myself against the door and fell to my knees, and Jub had to admit I was right, the man wasn't necessarily tall."

"He didn't plan it, either," Mitch said. "Taking the dagger from the wall like that, it figures spur of the moment stuff."

"Or else somebody who knew the dagger was always there."

Mitch shook his head. "Nothing's always there. When you plan a murder, you bring the weapon with you. You wouldn't take the chance that maybe she put the knife somewhere else, to clean it or show it off or something."

Then the doorbell rang and Gladys jumped up. "I'll answer it," she said.

Mitch turned to Amy and they exchanged a look. Amy had kind of engineered the Freeman marriage and she felt like she owned it. Every time she saw the pair of them together, she acted like she was still at the wedding.

When Jub came in, she held out her two hands. Jub didn't know what to do with them, so he grabbed the nearest one and said, "Hi, you look pretty good." Then he said hello to Mitch and Mitch told him to sit down and let somebody bring him a beer.

Jub grinned and the dimple crossed his cheek. His face was a little puffy from the heat and he had a tired look to him, and when he sat down, he unlaced his shoes and kicked them off. He took a long gulp of the beer that Gladys brought him. Then Glad went out to the kitchen to fuss around with Amy.

"How's it going?" Mitch asked.

Jub sighed. "Too much to do," he said. "We have stuff we haven't even touched. I've gone over most of the physical

110

evidence, but the rest of the gang are still running ragged. For instance, she was mixed up with a real-estate operator named Marlin. Business, social, a little of each."

"I heard something about him," Mitch said.

"High-powered operator with the gift of gab. Has a girl and brother act working for him, and he has them hypnotized. The brother, Ben Browne, is a smoothie of an accountant, and the girl's a tart who ropes in the customers. Susceptible old men, mostly, with the dough."

"Bill got anything on them?" Mitch asked.

"Hasn't had time yet, but you know how he operates. Soften up his suspects and act as if he believed every word, and let them go. Then check up and call them back, and bang!"

"He can bang all right," Mitch remarked. "What about Drury? Where does he figure?"

"Drury's okay. Alibi, no motive. He's really broken up over Vixen. Chief trouble with him is he likes everybody too much, all he tells is how nice they are. He admits Marlin's sharp, but says he's the salt of the earth, and he insists that this Browne girl is as pure as his own daughter. You can't tell by looks, he says."

"Boy!" Mitch said. "Can't you, though! But if Drury's so damn nice, what about his wife? He two-timed her, didn't he? She had to go out and hire a detective." He took another sip of beer. "And what about that guy Greenleaf, huh?"

"He's clean. He came in by himself and told us all he knew. He made a little trouble about turning over his reports, but Mrs. Drury had a complete file and Bill saw them."

"Yeah," said Mitch. "You know, when I was at the Vixen house with Ed, I noticed a probation manual. Funny thing to find in *her* house, wasn't it?"

"I had it in the lab and couldn't get a thing out of it, the way it was all chewed up. Somebody must have thrown it away long ago."

"Yeah," said Mitch. He sipped his beer contentedly and

felt good. They'd passed up Greenleaf one hundred per cent, so Greenleaf was still his baby. All his.

A slight smile played at the corner of Mitch's lips, and he sighed. A guy can dream, anyhow. He looked up at Jub and saw that Jub was woolgathering, too. For a second, it hit Mitch that maybe Jub was onto the same thing.

"What is it, Jub?"

Jub kind of jerked. "Thinking," he said, with a frown. "Something came up this afternoon, Bill thinks he may crack this case pretty soon."

"Who?" Mitch asked.

"Edith Drury."

"Wow!" Mitch said. "Her?"

Jub nodded, and Mitch's mind began to work. "She's got a motive all right, but what about opportunity? Can you pin her down to the Vixen house?"

"Not yet. She claims she was home all day Sunday until around five, but the funny thing is the maid didn't see her for quite a while. And Drury called California and spoke to their daughter. We checked with her and she said she asked to talk to her mother and Drury said she was out."

"What does Drury say to that?"

"That he doesn't remember his exact words, he thinks he just said Mrs. Drury wasn't there. He wanted a quiet chat with his daughter, alone, and didn't want Mrs. Drury in on it."

"Stuff like that," Mitch said, "you never really get it straight." He let his mind empty out, so that the idea of Mrs. Drury would have more room. "What's she like?" he asked presently.

"Well, she bossed the whole Homicide Squad around, and when Ed lit up a cigar, you should have heard her bawl him out."

"Them cigars of his," Mitch said. "I wish I could have seen him. She sat on him good, huh?"

"With that kind of temper, she's certainly capable of taking a dagger and stabbing somebody she hates. And believe me, she hates."

"Which is why she hired a detective."

"Sure," Jub said. "But the strange thing is, she claims she wasn't thinking of a divorce, and Greenleaf backs her up on that."

"Then what did she hire him for?"

"I don't know," Jub said, "and I'm not even sure that she understands her own reasons. She kept building up evidence, but she wasn't planning on a divorce. What she was really after—it's hard to say."

"Makes no sense," Mitch said. "She must have wanted a divorce and just wasn't ready for it. Or else she was building up for something she never got around to, but would have. Anyhow, if she did it, how did she get into the house? Vixen wouldn't let her in, not for anything."

"Door was unlocked. Always was. We couldn't even find a key."

"Well," Mitch said, seeing Greenleaf slip away from him. "First you got to prove she was there."

"Have to take it easy, too. The Drury connections go right up to the Commissioner's office." Jub finished his beer. "Well, there you have it, Mitch. Outside of the Marlin angle, Edith Drury's the big play. You'll probably be working on it tomorrow checking taxis, bus drivers, anybody who might have seen her. Bill's going all out."

Amy's voice, behind Mitch, came sharp and clear. "How old is she, Jub? Mrs. Drury, that is."

"Late forties. Why?"

"I was thinking that at her age, with change of life problems and then losing her husband, she could get awfully desperate. Glad and I were just talking about her. It sounds right."

"I think it is right," Jub said, "but it's going to be tough to prove. Because there's the evidence that someone drank a glass of orange juice, and no lipstick, remember. And then someone made those marks on the wall with his feet, and the person was not Edith Drury. And I can so testify, from the marks."

113

H

Mitch didn't argue, but it hit him that even if Greenleaf hadn't committed the murder, he could still be important. Naturally, Mitch would be a lot better off if Greenleaf had done the job, but that wasn't up to Mitch. The thing was, he had Greenleaf on the hook and he ought to use him.

After dinner, Mitch went downstairs with Jub. Jub was due back at headquarters and Mitch said. "You using your car tonight?"

"Just to go over to the lab. Want it?"

"I could use it. I'll drop you off first, huh?"

That was how Mitch happened to go up to Raffneyville.

On the way he dropped in at that Gulf station, he figured maybe he could get the guy there to say Drury had stopped for gas a lot earlier than anybody thought, which would make Greenleaf a liar and leave him wide open, no alibi at all.

Naturally, Mitch didn't put his questions right off. He shot the breeze a little, to bring the guy around. But this pump-handle, you couldn't lead him, he wouldn't give with a statement. He said he'd been so busy that Sunday he didn't know where he was at, and the cops were pretty lucky that Drury'd used a credit card, otherwise Drury would have been lost in the crowd.

Mitch thanked the guy for nothing and kept on up to Raffneyville. He hit the village all right and he went into this crowded hick bar to get directions, but they must have all been plastered because what they told him was cockeyed and he never did find the Marlin place. He went around in circles, and by the time he knew where he was, he was half-way back to town.

What the hell, he figured. He might as well give up and go home.

He trudged in around midnight, feeling that Greenleaf had played a dirty trick on him and he'd make Greenleaf sweat for it. The guy belonged to him, he was Mitch's pigeon, so where the hell did he get off, double-crossing Mitch and walking out on him?

Mitch sat down in the big chair. He heard Mamie crying in her room, and Amy's soothing voice telling her it was all right, go on back to sleep.

After a little while, Amy came in. She had that bright look on her, not just her face, it was all over her and made her look like a slice of rainbow. She was different from anybody he'd ever come across and sometimes he got a little dizzy, just being near her.

"Mamie all right?" he asked.

"Yes. She had a nightmare and woke up. Poor thing, she can't stand the heat."

Amy came over to the chair and sat down on the arm. "What is it, Mitchel?" she asked.

"Nothing."

"There is something."

"Yeah," he said. It was funny how Amy could look inside him and pull out whatever she was after. Sometimes it was what he was thinking, and sometimes she got hold of a piece of him that made his eyes shine, like he was hearing the angels sing. You never knew.

"Amy," he said, "maybe Edith Drury killed her, but suppose I had hold of the key to the whole business, something right in front of their noses, but the boys passed it up, so far. It could put me right back on the Homicide Squad, maybe."

Amy ruffled Mitch's hair, gently. "Wouldn't it be better to go straight to Bill Decker and tell him? The trouble you had with him was always because you tried to do things your way, and not his."

"I got to wrap this up right, first. Amy, can you see me walking into his office and sitting down and saying, kind of quiet, 'Excuse me, Lieutenant, but if you're not too busy, I got the Vivian Vixen killer outside. He just confessed.' Then the lieutenant, he'll do a kind of double take, but he'll know I'm giving it to him straight. And he's one guy that won't try to cover up and then hog all the medals." Mitch's hand found Amy's and squeezed it. "Not him," Mitch said, with a kind of pride. "Not him. Never."

Amy leaned over, and her lips brushed Mitch's forehead. "Dreamer," she said. "Hero, riding a big white horse and discovering truth all by yourself."

"I'm not much," he said. "But somehow, I like to do things myself."

She eased off the arm of the chair and slid down. "Mitchell," she said, "hadn't you better pull down the shade?"

"Sure," he said. But he didn't move. How in hell can you get up and pull down the shade, when you got a wife in your lap?

10

IT HAD RAINED some during the night and cooled things off a little, but you still knew it was summer and the heat still hurt. Mitch, starting off the day's patrol with Oscar, drove slow and easy along the residential blocks.

He had a couple of ideas on how he was going to squeeze Greenleaf, but the thing was, Mitch had to stop in at Greenleaf's office to start the ball rolling. It would be a little silly for Mitch to go there on his own time, so he had to do some preparing. After a while, he had an angle.

"You notice that thing on the bulletin-board about a car operating without a muffler?" he remarked. "Woke up this Mrs. Winkler in the middle of the night."

"Crank stuff," Oscar said. "What about it?"

"I dunno," Mitch said. "I figured maybe we'd stop in there and get the details."

"Are you nuts?" Oscar asked in surprise.

"You never can tell," Mitch said mildly. A crank like that, you could easily feed her an idea and she'd say sure, it must

116

be so-and-so's car, and then Mitch would say he'd check on so-and-so's license, and then he'd call the sergeant for permission to go down to headquarters, and Greenleaf's office was right around the corner. So Mitch said, "It don't hurt to talk to her."

"Waste of time," Oscar said. "What are you really after, Mitch?"

"Nothing much," Mitch said.

He swung into Hawthorne, where there were a few shops and a gas station. He was in the inside lane and still dawdling along when he saw a big guy step out of a car. He was carrying a suit on his arm, and he crossed the sidewalk and went into a cleaning store. Mitch stopped immediately and pulled over to the curb.

"That's him," Mitch said. "Greenleaf, this joker I was telling about."

"So what?" Oscar said. "He can get a suit cleaned, can't he?"

"Sure," said Mitch. "Only I want to look at that suit."

Oscar laughed. "What do you expect to find? Bloodstains?"

Mitch rolled his shoulders uncomfortably, and Oscar said, "You're off your rocker. Does a guy wait three days and then decide to get rid of the blood on his clothes?"

"Who mentioned blood?" Mitch demanded. "Not me, did I?"

"I'm a mind reader," said Oscar. He peered through the wind-shield and said, "He's coming out now."

"Yeah," said Mitch. He watched Greenleaf leave the store and turn to the right. A few doors away, Greenleaf went into another shop.

"Florist," Oscar observed. "Buying flowers for his girl, I guess."

"Him?" said Mitch. "He wouldn't part with a buck except to fill his own belly."

"Take it easy," Oscar said. "Don't let him get your goat."

"Me?" said Mitch. "I'm just interested. And if this wagon

117

wasn't pasted with police signs, I'd follow along and see where he goes."

"He's coming out now," Oscar said. "And he didn't buy any flowers."

Mitch's eyes followed Greenleaf as he reached the sidewalk and headed back briskly. But apparently Greenleaf didn't notice the police car. He stopped in front of the gray, shabby-looking job that he'd parked, and he climbed in. A few seconds later, he swung out into the traffic and drove off.

"May as well check up on him," Mitch remarked, and stepped out.

He went into the cleaning establishment first and said to a red-headed girl with glasses, "Somebody just brought a suit in here. Mind if I have a look at it?"

She acted a little scared at seeing a cop, but she was anxious to please. She said, "Why, yes," and handed Mitch a light tan suit.

While Mitch examined it, he said, "What did he want done?"

"Just cleaned. He said there was no hurry."

"I see." Mitch moved a little so the light would be better. "He give his name?"

"It's there, on the ticket."

Mitch saw the slip of paper pinned to it. "J. Smith," he read. He went over the suit inch by inch. There were some old-looking stains, nothing to get excited about. Then he saw the tear in the pants.

"Did he want this repaired?" he asked.

"He didn't mention it."

"I see. If he says he's in no hurry, I guess he won't be around for a while."

"He said he might not be in for a few weeks."

"Yeah," Mitch said. This was as good a way as any to get rid of a piece of evidence. Leave it in a cleaning shop under a fake name, and then forget about it.

He put the suit down. "Maybe you'll do me a little favor and put this aside. I'll be around in a couple of days. Okay?"

"Of course." Her eyes grew bigger and she wanted to ask what this was all about, but she didn't have the nerve. Mitch said, "Thanks, Miss," and went out. He figured things were shaping up, but he didn't have much time to think, because he had to find out about the flowers, next.

The florist was a little guy with a little black mustache and with pint-sized hands built just right for handling forget-me-nots and tying up violets.

"You got a nice place here," Mitch said. "Cool, too."

"If she's no cool, the flowers alla die."

"Yeah," said Mitch. "This big guy who was just in here. What did he want?"

"No buy," the florist said. "He ask a lotta questions. He's a cop, no? He gotta the badge."

"No cop," Mitch said. He didn't go into that one too deep. Better save it, he thought, and said, "Questions? What about?"

"About the ribbon. He wanta find the shop where they have a lavender-and-yellow ribbon to tie up the flower. Then he aska me if I sell the orchid on Saturday or Sunday."

"Orchids?" Mitch said. "What for? What was he getting at?"

The florist shrugged. Mitch said, "Any time you want a favor, you let me know, huh? Taylor's the name. Now this guy who impersonated an officer—you understand what that means, huh?"

"Sure, sure. Only all he do is—"

"Never mind about that," Mitch said. "I'm here to protect you against guys that stick their nose in your business and then want to step on you later on. So if he showed you a badge and made you think he was a cop, that's impersonation, and I may want you to sign a complaint." He grinned. "But not unless I have to, because you're okay, Mister. I'll be seeing you."

He left jauntily and got back in the car. Oscar said, "Find out anything?"

Mitch eased out into the traffic. "Well, he gave a fake name

119

at the cleaner's, and he's asking about orchids tied up in a lavender-and-yellow ribbon. Any idea what florist that would be?" Oscar shook his head and Mitch went on. "Where do we find the next one?"

"On Clemens, I guess. Think this is hooked up with the Vixen case?"

"I don't know," Mitch said, "But when that big bastard asks questions, he's onto something."

"And a fake name," Oscar said. "What would he do that for?"

"Blood," Mitch said, chuckling. "You called it yourself."

"See any stains?"

Mitch shook his head. "It's the orchid stuff that has me guessing."

"Maybe it wasn't his suit," Oscar said.

Mitch snorted, and drove on at a nice, comfortable pace.

He reached the store on Clemens just in time to see Greenleaf's gray buggy leaving. But inside the shop, Mitch found out nothing more than he'd learned at the first place. Greenleaf was asking if anybody had bought an orchid corsage tied with a lavender-and-yellow ribbon.

Thoughtfully, Mitch returned to the car. "Where's the next one?" he asked.

Oscar objected. "Mitch, we stick to the regular rounds. When we pass a florist, we can stop, but we don't want to chase around and be way over on the wrong side of the precinct if something happens. Because that can be no good."

"Sure," Mitch said. "You got more sense than me, Oscar. Let's move." He made a U-turn and was back on the beat when the despatcher buzzed them. Oscar picked up the phone and answered.

"Henderson, Car Seven-Four."

A dry, clear monotone sounded through the phone. "Proceed to headquarters where Taylor will leave the car and report to Lieutenant Decker, Homicide, for special duty. Henderson, you will then continue to patrol alone, covering your usual area. Please acknowledge."

"Okay, Sergeant. Taylor to report to Homicide, and then I take over alone. We're on our way."

He replaced the phone. Mitch let out a low whistle and headed downtown.

"I wonder what that's about," Oscar said.

"I can make a pretty good guess. They're short-handed, and they're closing in." Mitch slowed at the next intersection, saw there was no traffic, and jumped the light. "Edith Drury," he said.

"No kidding?" Oscar said. He sounded excited. "Where'd you hear that?"

"Jub Freeman told me last night."

Mitch drove fast expertly. He used the siren only once, when he swung into the opposite lane to get by a long line of traffic.

He stopped in front of the Seagrave Building. "I'll leave you here, Oscar. Got to see a man about something, first. Take it easy." He hopped out and went into the lobby.

Greenleaf was listed in 1010, and Mitch took the elevator up and went into one of those big offices where six or eight guys rent space and use the same switchboard. The girl operating it looked like she ate too much candy.

"Hank Greenleaf in?" Mitch asked her.

"No. He was here for his mail this morning, and then he left. He didn't say when he'd be back."

Mitch nodded and gave her a long, level stare. "I figured he'd be out," he said. "Look, I wonder whether—" He stopped and shook his head. He could see her getting curious.

"Is there anything I can do?" she asked. She gave him her best smile, which wasn't too good.

Mitch considered her request as if he had to make up his mind whether she was worthy. He kept her waiting on purpose before he said, frowning. "He ever tell you anything about the Vixen case?"

With the mention of the Vixen case, he had her hooked. She said, "No, but he knows Mr. Drury, and Mrs. Drury was

121

here in the office once, but Hank won't even talk about them."

"He's got his reasons," Mitch said. "Now, I don't like to ask a nice kid like you to do anything you don't want to, but—" He let the sentence trail off, and he turned around and studied the row of filing cabinets.

"You mean he's involved?" she asked, and her eyes were popping. "No wonder he wouldn't tell me anything."

"You catch on fast," Mitch said. "You say you want to help out, huh?"

"With the Vixen case?"

"Sure. So any messages Greenleaf gets, maybe you can make a note of them. And if you happened to listen in on his calls and you heard something, you'd tell me, huh?"

"I—I don't know. Would it be right?"

"I'll protect you, don't worry about that."

Then the switchboard buzzed and she picked up a wire and started to answer. Mitch said, "Okay, sister. You do that." He went out and took the elevator down and walked to headquarters.

Bill Decker had a thin girl at the desk in the outer office where Gladys used to sit, and Mitch told this cookie who he was, while he looked her over. She was a brunette with good eyes and a nice voice, and she picked up the phone and spoke to Decker and then told Mitch to wait.

A couple of patrolmen from the Sixth were sitting there and Mitch began chewing the fat with them. He found out they were here for the same reason as himself, Decker needed them for special duty, and after a couple of minutes Decker's door swung open and he called out, "The three of you—come in."

Decker's office was familiar enough to Mitch. It was still too small for all the junk in it, the stuffed crocodile was still there on a shelf, and the desk was a mess of scraps of papers, bits of envelopes and assorted folders.

Decker squeaked back in his swivel-chair, and it hadn't been oiled yet. He treated Mitch just like the two others, and Mitch sat down on a high stool and pretended he'd never seen the lieutenant before.

"We think we got a break in the case," the lieutenant said, with fire in his eyes. "But brother, we could be awful wrong. So don't shoot off your mouths, and if a reporter grabs you on the way out, tell him you're going across the street for a cheeseburger, and that you don't like cheese."

One of the patrolmen laughed and the other one gave with a wide smile. Mitch rolled his shoulders and looked bored.

"Here's what," Decker said, as if he was handing out a couple of citations. "We think Mrs. Drury went out of the house before twelve-thirty. She denies it, and if we can prove she's a liar, we'll really pile it on. We've got to work fast, and that's where you come in.

"We think she went to Vivian Vixen's. She didn't take her car, she didn't take a taxi, and it was too far to walk in that heat. That makes it a bus, and Number Fourteen runs from her corner and passes Bierce and Hawthorne, where she'd get off."

The two patrolmen nodded and tried to look important, Mitch didn't.

"We've checked all the Number Fourteen drivers that could have taken her, and none of them remembers her, which is par for the course. The only thing they don't forget is to take your token."

The phone rang and Decker picked it up, muttered into it, then nodded and scrawled something on a printed slip of paper that looked like an unpaid milk bill. He slapped the phone back in its cradle.

"That leaves the bus passengers. On a half-empty bus on Sunday, passengers would notice her, and we've got to locate one of them. You—" Decker pointed to the guy who'd smiled—"check the congregation of the Lutheran church, the sermon was over at noon and some of the worshippers probably took the Number Fourteen bus home. You—" the lieutenant pointed to the guy who'd laughed—"check the Bierce Street area for maids who rode that bus going to

work on Sunday between eleven and three. The girl outside
has lists for you, and some pictures of Mrs. Drury. You—"
Decker nodded at Mitch—"same thing. Divide up the area
between you. That's all."

The three patrolmen stood up, and the guys from the Sixth
went out. Mitch stayed there, looking bothered.

"Well?" Decker said.

"Lieutenant, I got kind of an idea. This Greenleaf who
was tailing Drury, he didn't pick Drury up until noon, so
Greenleaf should have been waiting in front of the apartment. If Mrs. Drury came out before Greenleaf left, he saw
her."

"I spoke to him and he didn't see anybody."

"She was his employer," Mitch said earnestly, "so he
wouldn't get her in trouble. I know that guy, Lieutenant,
and he's tricky. But he was right there outside the Drury
apartment, and I figure I can maybe make him talk. And
anyhow, now that it's important, he could change his mind
and give out. You know how it is."

Decker opened his mouth and took in a big breath.
"Brother!" he said in a low voice. "I think you got something."

"I could look him up," Mitch said.

"Friend of yours?"

"Well, I know him," Mitch said modestly. "And I ought to
be able to locate him."

Decker nodded. "All right. Go ahead."

Mitch walked out, deciding he'd go up to Greenleaf's
office and park for a while. Which was a hell of a lot better
than tramping around in the heat. So whatever happened,
he was on top.

He told the guy from the Sixth that he'd have to work
alone. "Lieutenant changed his mind," Mitch said. The guy
looked a little sore and Mitch turned away. That was when
Ed Balenky came out of the squad room and said hello.

"On my way to the washroom," he said. "What's with you,
Mitch?"

124

Mitch fell into step. "The lieutenant's up against it," he said. "When he wants to check a whole congregation to find out somebody that rode a bus—boy, that's fighting the odds."

"I never saw a case with so much detail to it," Balenky said. He shoved open the door of the washroom. "There's all those movies of hers to look at, for instance, and the chance of turning something up. Twelve Hollywood pictures and about fourteen hours of her own stuff, home movies. Shots of Raffneyville and shots of friends of hers. You never know what you might find."

"Yeah," said Mitch, sighing. But automatically his mind made a fast survey, how he could maybe have wangled the job of watching movies all day, if he'd still been on the Homicide Squad. "Who's looking at them?" he asked.

"Joe. I tried to tell the boss how I was the man that could do it, but he picks Joe."

"You didn't play it right," Mitch said. "What you shoulda done is, you say you know a friend of hers, he can maybe put name tags on some of the faces, and then you pick somebody that knew her and you bring him along with you."

"Boss wouldn't fall for that."

Mitch shrugged. "Worth a try, Ed. Just sitting there and looking at movies all day—that would be the life, huh?"

Balenky dried his hands. "I don't know. Gets your eyes all tired out, and when the optic nerve is strained, you don't sleep good."

"Wouldn't bother me none," Mitch announced. He looked at himself in the mirror and made a face. "You think Edith Drury's really the end of the line?"

"How do I know?" Ed started to leave the washroom, and then stopped. "But I'll tell you, Mitch. I ran into something else, it's just opening up." He turned around and looked at the row of closed doors, like there were usually a couple of Russian spies sitting on the can. "Mitch, did you know that Drury gave Vixen a check for three-thousand bucks? And that she went to the bank and cashed it?"

"What happened to it?"

"Here's what," Balenky said, confidentially. "According to Drury, she paid it to Marlin, to buy a house. According to Marlin, he never got it. According to me, she still had the dough on Sunday and the guy that killed her picked it up and walked off with it. Three grand, and hot."

Mitch's mind spoke. It said Greenleaf.

The hitch was, how do you prove Greenleaf had that three grand? Mitch needed a court order to find out if Greenleaf had banked it, and that was something Mitch couldn't get. He was just a patrolman kind of kibitzing in on the case.

He took the problem with him across the street, where he had lunch at the Greek's that Amy said had bum food. He saw some of the Homicide boys and he kidded around, and when he left, he more or less had the problem solved.

Bluff it, he told himself. Act like he'd got the court order and knew Greenleaf had banked the wad. If Greenleaf hadn't banked it, he'd be pretty sure of himself. Mitch would know.

He went back to the Seagrave Building and up to the tenth, and this girl was still at the switchboard. Mitch asked her if any calls had come in and she said just one, from his garage, so Mitch said okay, he'd stick around and wait for Greenleaf, and any calls that came in, Mitch would take them. He'd be in Greenleaf's office.

"It's locked," she said.

"Well, ask the super to come up. He'll let me in."

"I can call him," the girl said, "but Hank has strict orders never to let anyone in without him. And besides," she added, busting into a grin, "everything inside's locked."

Mitch grinned back at her. "I guess I'll wait," he said.

He sat there thinking of the those movies, and then his mind went blank and nothing much registered, except that if Greenleaf had got a call, Mitch would have known it and been on his feet saying he'd take it.

But nothing happened. Maybe an hour went by, a nice, easy sixty minutes, and then the door opened and there was

Greenleaf. He looked like he was dead-beat, and he stopped short and kind of glared at Mitch and didn't say anything.

Mitch stood up. "Hello," he said. "I missed you last night."

"I was out of town," Greenleaf said, like he knew he'd had that appointment at the bar and wasn't going to try and weasel out of it.

"Where?" said Mitch.

"You know damn well where I was," Greenleaf snapped out. "What do you want now?"

"Let's me and you go into your office," Mitch said.

Greenleaf led the way and unlocked the door. It wasn't much of an office and the partitions reached the ceiling and whoever was next door could hear every word, which was a hell of a place for a guy whose business could be private.

Greenleaf sat down without offering Mitch a chair, so Mitch parked on the edge of the desk where he could look down instead of up.

"What's this about?" Greenleaf demanded.

Mitch eyed him a few seconds before saying, "Let's get something straight, between the two of us. If you box around or if you give me any phony information, I'm going to pull you in, fast. You'll go right up to the Fourteenth and you'll be in a back room and you won't be happy. After that you'll be in the middle of more trouble than you ever heard of, and I ain't kidding."

"Nuts!" Greenleaf said. "What the hell could you charge me with?"

"Obstruction of justice, on account of you're holding out material evidence."

"Get out!" Greenleaf said in a low voice. "You haven't even the right to ask a question, and you know it. The guy who's going to be in trouble—that's you."

"Yeah?" said Mitch. "Just pick up the phone and call Homicide. Get the chief and ask him if I got authority to interrogate. Go ahead."

Greenleaf picked up the phone and dialed. Mitch heard him say, "Homicide Squad," then, "Lieutenant Decker?

127

Greenleaf. There's an officer here named Taylor. Does he have any authority to question me?"

Greenleaf pressed the receiver tight against his ear, and he blushed slowly. Then he put the phone down and looked at Mitch. "What do you want to know?" he asked Mitch.

"I want to know why you killed her."

Greenleaf grunted. "That stuff doesn't go," he said. "Not around here."

"Impersonating an officer," Mitch said.

That took the laugh off Greenleaf's face. "What do you mean by that?"

"All those florists." Mitch raised the pitch of his voice until it squeaked with sarcasm. "Who bought the orchids, Hank boy?"

"What orchids?"

"You had a badge and impersonated an officer, and I got at least one guy who's willing to swear to it. On a warrant."

"How much did you pay him?"

"Then there's the suit you left at the cleaner's. Under the name of Smith. Want to give me the ticket for it?"

"What suit?" Greenleaf asked, but even Mamie would have caught on he was stalling.

"The one with the tear in the pants. Ripped it at her place, didn't you?" Greenleaf clamped his lips shut, and Mitch said, "About that license of yours, private investigator. You want to hang onto it, don't you?"

"The hell with the license," Greenleaf said.

"And all that dough you banked. Vixen had plenty around, on Sunday, and what happened to it? So there's a larceny charge, too."

"The money I banked," Greenleaf began angrily, and then cut himself off.

Mitch said, "Yeah? Three thousand, wasn't it?"

Greenleaf looked like he'd been caught with his pants down, and Mitch figured the sap had gone and put the dough in the bank. In a way, Mitch was surprised, he'd thought Greenleaf was a lot smarter.

"So that's how it is," Mitch said. "Now about those orchids—"

"Had nothing to do with Vixen," Greenleaf snapped.

"Then," Mitch said, "there's that kid of yours. Funny things happen to a kid when the cops get hold of him."

"What the hell are you talking about?" Greenleaf demanded.

Mitch let him have it. "Your alibi. You went swimming with your kid when you claim you were out in Raffneyville, or on the way back."

"Who said that?"

"So we ask him a few questions, see? And your own kid— *he* breaks that alibi of yours."

"You little son of a bitch!" said Greenleaf, in a tight, jerky voice.

Mitch nodded. "That's me. I never let up, Hank boy. I keep pushing it."

Greenleaf pumped up and made a pass at Mitch. The way Greenleaf shot forward, he was off-balance and couldn't hit out, he just tried to grab Mitch and set him up. Mitch twisted and rapped Greenleaf's arm hard, where it hurt. Greenleaf let out a grunt and stood up, springy on his feet and looking for an opening.

Mitch ducked fast. He was no match for the big guy, he knew he'd get beat up, so he yanked out his gun and jumped back against the wall. When Greenleaf saw the gun, he stopped. He kind of muttered something about putting the gun down and he took a deep breath, and his face looked like he'd splotched it up with red paint.

The way Greenleaf hated him the other night, that was nothing. Here was one guy who'd knock Mitch off if he had half a chance, and love it. But the guy didn't have the chance and he saw the gun, so he took some deep breaths and kind of shook his head, and then he sat down heavy. Mitch pocketed his gun.

"I guess we know where we stand," Mitch said. He was on top now, so he rubbed it in a little. "Funny thing," he remarked. "Over at Homicide, they don't know about you, they think you're okay."

"You tell 'em," Greenleaf mumbled.

"I'll tell 'em when I'm ready. Right now they got another idea, and that's what they sent me over for. Look, Hank boy—what time did you see Mrs. Drury leave the house on Sunday?"

Greenleaf gulped. "Mrs. Drury?" he said in surprise. "Where does she come in?"

"Just tell me. What time. You were waiting in front of the house when she came out. What time?"

"I don't know anything about her."

"That's what you told the lieutenant. Look, just think of your kid a little, and then think of how you impersonated an officer. I can step on you right now, or I can hold off for a while. No promises, but you can do yourself a favor, huh?"

Greenleaf's face worked, and he bit his lips and stared out the window. He swung around suddenly. "If you want to know—sure. No reason why I should hold out. I was waiting across the street from her apartment. She came out at eleven forty-five, and she walked down to the corner bus stop. She got on the first one that came along."

"Then what?"

"Then nothing. I waited for Drury."

"Yeah," said Mitch. "Now about those orchids, and the lavender-and-yellow ribbon. You want to tell me about it now, or you want I should let the lieutenant sweat it out of you?"

"That's another investigation," Greenleaf said. "Nothing to do with Vixen."

"We can check that ribbon easy," Mitch said. "We got a collection of florist ribbons, all I got to do is pick the right one, and then go see the guy."

Greenleaf dropped one of his big paws on the desk. "I hear you came up to Raffneyville last night. What for?"

"To see you," Mitch said. "Only the directions they gave me—boy, I never even got there."

"You got there," Greenleaf said in a low voice. "I saw you."

"No kiddin'. What was I doing?"

"I'm going to hang it on you," Greenleaf said angrily. "How much was Vivian paying you?"

"Me? What would she pay me for?"

"Those movies. Those private showings."

"Oh." This was news to Mitch, and it explained why she'd paid off so easy. He wondered what the boys would say when they got around to those films. Maybe they'd let Mitch in on it, he'd have to see Ed and put in his bid.

"You seem to know plenty," Mitch said. And Greenleaf gave him a crooked smile and said, "I know she paid you a hundred bucks for protection. Because she put it down in her private account book."

"Nuts," said Mitch. He didn't even blink, but he was plenty worried. The guy with the dark hair must have kept that hundred and Mitch was hooked.

It always worked out like that. No matter how careful you were, it was the other stuff that banged down on you. A lousy ham sandwich, a gigolo with itchy fingers—you were clean as a whistle, and then, socko!

Nevertheless Mitch looked cheerful and unbothered as he went to the door.

"See you tonight," he said. "At the bar, huh?" And he turned around and went out.

11

AFTER TAYLOR HAD gone, Hank went out to the switchboard to check on any calls. Libby gave him a smile that almost lifted her out of her chair.

"Oh, Hank, I'm so glad you're still here. I heard what you

said, he threatened you with a gun, didn't he? I thought he was going to arrest you."

"You did? What gave you that idea?"

"The way he was waiting, before you got here. And he was here earlier and told me you were involved in the Vixen case, and would I help."

"What did he say? What did he want you to do?"

"To listen in on your calls, and then tell him. But Hank, I wouldn't do that, it wouldn't be right. And now tell me about Vivian Vixen."

"I never even met her," Hank said, and went back to his office.

There, he sat down and put his head in his hands. Again, as on and off all day, he was obsessed with the picture of Celia's body lying, undiscovered, in Vivian's room. A slow, smoldering anger burned through Hank's mind and he felt indecent, inhuman, almost guilty of betrayal.

The initial shock of her death, however, had worn off, and Hank was reasonably certain of what must have happened. Someone had broken into Vivian's room last night. Celia, who slept near it, had heard a noise and gone to investigate. And the intruder had killed her.

Furthermore, Taylor fitted the role of the intruder. He had opportunity, and he had a motive for wanting bribery evidence. He was trying to frame Hank, and if a button had dropped off Hank's jacket while he'd been with Taylor, Taylor would use it. In exactly this way.

After a while, Hank picked up the phone and called Jean at Lake Pride. With trouble ahead, he wanted to have his family with him, and Toby in particular. Maybe he could explain to Toby that their swim last Sunday was a secret, although that had to be done cautiously, without letting Toby think he was being asked to lie.

To Jean, Hank merely said he had to keep expenses down and wanted to give up the cottage. He asked her to arrange it, and he promised to call tomorrow. Then Hank leaned back and tried to assess his position with Taylor.

Hank was on shaky ground, and up against a guy who was as shrewd as he was ruthless. What it amounted to was a race between them. Whoever nailed the other one first would win, and the stakes were a murder charge.

Hank had to admit that Taylor was doing all right. For evidence, Taylor had a civil-service manual, a pair of ripped pants, the orchid clue. But his ace in the hole was the knowledge that Hank had in fact been at the Vixen house.

Hank fingered a pencil and then tapped the end of it on his desk. When Taylor had been here, Hank had deliberately given the impression that he'd taken Vivian's missing three-thousand and put it in the bank. Let Taylor act on the impression, and he'd fall flat on his face. Hank almost smiled at the prospect, until it struck him that if Taylor had believed him, Taylor hadn't stolen it, either.

Somehow, every time Hank thought he had the guy in a hole, Taylor climbed out. He was making an unauthorized investigation, but Lieutenant Decker backed him up and blasted Hank's eardrums just for having doubts. Taylor had taken a bribe from Vivian, but the only evidence was a vague and unreliable statement on the part of Ben Browne. Taylor had been in Raffneyville on the night of Celia's death, but officially, there was no murder.

So how could Hank slap Taylor down? And more to the point, how could Hank do it without putting himself in the middle of the whole mess?

The answer was so simple and obvious that Hank swung around in his chair and let out a yelp. Enter a complaint against Taylor, demand a departmental examination. Hank would be called as a witness and he'd have his chance to tie Taylor into knots. When you accuse a cop of taking graft and of keeping evidence to himself, he's in trouble. Even if he clears himself, the smear sticks.

For the first time since he'd met Taylor, Hank felt hopeful. To celebrate, he left his office and crossed the street to the city hall. Forms for the next group of civil-service exams were stacked up in the clerk's office, and Hank found the one for parole officer. There was nothing on it that would force him to state he'd had his license as an investigator revoked, but there was a form attached for a couple of sponsors who had to sign an attestation of applicant's good moral character.

Maybe he'd ask Drury, after the Vixen business was over. Drury's name pulled weight, and he'd certainly be willing.

In a buoyant mood, Hank drove up to the Fourteenth Precinct station and parked his gray buggy in the lot. He had no trouble getting to see Pisani, and Hank made a formal complaint. He did not, however, tip his whole hand. He said that Taylor had threatened him with a gun, had attempted to interfere with the conduct of Hank's business, and forced Hank to submit to unauthorized questioning.

Pisani listened coldly. "You say he told this girl to listen in on your phone messages, and he pulled a gun. What's wrong with that?"

"I'll show it at the proper time. And a few other things, too."

"I hope you realize that when these alleged acts occurred, he was carrying out an assignment for the Homicide Squad. He wasn't even working under my orders."

"You're Taylor's boss, aren't you? Thats why I'm here."

"Exactly where do you get off, walking in and telling me to discipline one of my men?"

"What about all those questions in the bar the other night? Did you authorize him to investigate?"

"Who said he investigated?" Pisani asked. "You're throwing around some pretty big words, Greenleaf, and you claim he used force. Let me ask you something: In the bar there, you could get up and walk out any time you wanted to, couldn't you? Or did he try to stop you?"

"You can detain a man without using physical force, Lieutenant."

Pisani smiled coldly. "Greenleaf, take a little practical advice from somebody who knows his way around." He hunched forward over his desk and spoke confidentially.

"Why don't you tell me what Taylor's trying to find out? Then you'd really have him, wouldn't you?"

Hank didn't answer. Taylor must have planted the idea that Hank had knowledge more precious than rubies and emeralds, and the lieutenant wanted a sample. A small, red ruby, at least.

Hank got up stiffly and went out. He called the D.A.'s office from the nearest phone booth and asked for the detective bureau.

"George Anderson there?" he said. "I'd like to speak to him."

A moment later, a gruff voice came on. "Anderson, detective bureau."

"Andy, Hank Greenleaf speaking. I want to know where I stand on something, and I want it straight. If I come down and tell the D.A. a certain cop has been taking graft and is trying to frame me on a charge of impersonating an officer, what happens? Will I get action, or not?"

"Depends on who's involved. You know how things are, Hank."

"A patrolman named Mitchell Taylor. I spoke to Lieutenant Pisani and he gave me the run-around."

"Pisani doesn't pull much weight, Hank, and he's after a permanent appointment. Besides, the Fourteenth is for the dumb and the damned. Nobody there has any important connections."

"Thanks," Hank said. "I'll probably be down in the morning."

Then he went to see the Brownes.

They occupied the second-floor apartment of a converted, frame house. An upper verandah had been tacked onto the porch, and a kitchen and probably a bath had been added inside. The result was called an apartment.

Hank parked in front, but he didn't go in immediately. He'd been postponing this visit all day, ever since the stout clerk at Phil's Flower Shoppe had said, "Yes. I remember sending some orchids to a Bierce Street address, but I never

135

thought—" He looked unhappy and stuttered himself into silence.

"They went to Vivian Vixen," Hank said. "You didn't have the name?"

"No. Just a street address."

"Could I see the ribbon you use?"

The stout clerk pulled at the end of the yellow-and-lavender roll, and Hank nodded. "That's it. Who ordered them?"

"He didn't say. He just asked to have them sent, and he wrote out a card to go with them."

"What did he look like?"

The stout clerk hesitated so long that he seemed to be losing weight right in front of Hank's eyes. "You," he said finally.

Hank didn't bat an eye. "Like me?" he said. "You mean somebody who looked like me. Dark, my build. Is that it?"

The clerk nodded, but he might as well have said Ben Browne.

After that, Hank had gone back to his office, intending to think out his next move. Instead, he'd found Taylor.

Now, outside the Browne house, Hank sat at the wheel of the car. He'd traced the orchids so that he'd have something on Ben, and now Hank had it. And maybe Ben had stolen that three-thousand, too. So what was Hank worried about? Why sit here and dream up complications?

He got out of his car, walked up the path and mounted the stairs. He squinted at the square, hand printed card on the door. Browne. He rang the bell.

Liz, opening the door, showed a worried face that changed briefly into a broad smile of relief. "Oh, Hank!" she exclaimed. "I'm so glad you came." Then, raising her voice, she called out, "Ben, Hank's here. Isn't that wonderful?"

She led the way into a living room with comfortable, modernistic furniture. The walls were splashed with Liz's bold, vividly colored paintings.

Ben, holding a highball glass, obviously saw nothing wonderful about Hank. Ben said, "The police subpoenaed our books and took them away. They're probably working on them right now." Ben slapped down the highball glass and lowered his head in misery. He was almost sobbing. "Hank, they can put me in jail!"

Hank didn't answer. Liz put both hands on his arm and clutched it tight. Her eyes were weary, and he could tell she'd been crying.

"What are we going to do?" she asked. "Hank, you've got to help."

"Me? Where do I come in?"

"Take Ben away somewhere, save him."

Hank pulled back from Liz's imploring eyes. "How could I do that? And why should I?"

"Because it's not Ben's fault, he couldn't help it; they made him. He didn't do anything."

Hank turned to Ben. "No?" Hank said coldly, "Then why so scared of jail?"

Ben let out a groan. Liz stepped back and gave Hank an accusing look. Then she apparently voted for sweetness and light, and she crossed the room to a small bar and poured something from a decanter "Soda?" she said in a voice that dripped with honey and bubble-gum. "Or on the rocks?"

"On the rocks."

She brought over the drink, and Hank swished the ice around before tasting. "Thanks," he said. "But I didn't come here to do any favors."

"Hank," Liz said in a voice she might have used if she were lying next to him in bed. "If this is something unpleasant, don't say it. I've had enough troubles for one day."

The bedroom tone annoyed Hank. "So have I," he said brusquely. He stepped in front of Liz and, excluding her from the conversation, he spoke to Ben. "I found out who sent the orchids. The clerk at Phil's flower shop identified you."

Ben sat up, reached for his glass and began playing with it. "Anything wrong with sending flowers?" he asked.

137

"You thought so, otherwise you wouldn't have tried to get them back. And then, when you lost your nerve, sent Liz."

"Liz took them?" Ben said, smiling.

"Please," Liz said sharply. "Let's be honest with Hank."

Hank retreated and sat down. "Thanks, Liz. Curiously, what hurts most is, I kept telling myself that you liked me. Even though you really thought I might be involved, it didn't make any difference. I told myself you were generous and trusting in a world full of suspicious people. Now I find out that you've been playing me for a sucker. You knew the body was there and knew I couldn't possibly have killed her. You came on purpose to get those orchids."

"Of course I did, but how does that—"

"Liz!" Ben exclaimed angrily. "Shut up! The guy's trying to bleed you, every time you open your mouth you admit something a cop would give his right arm to hear."

Liz blinked and looked hurt. Hank said to Ben, "She's not telling me anything I don't know, or that the cops couldn't find out in two two seconds flat. I came to tell you I was willing to shut up about the orchids, but now I'm not so sure. With all the fancy lying going on, how can I trust either of you?"

"You better trust us," Ben said. "Otherwise—" He drew his hand across his throat and smiled malevolently.

"Go ahead," Hank said brusquely. "I didn't take three-thousand dollars from Vivian, and then hold it out on the guy I was working for. I don't have any motive, but you have. Larceny, Ben. Covering up a larceny."

Ben stood up. "That's right," he said. He staggered past Hank, almost fell, and managed to prop himself against a table. He fumbled with the table drawer. "What are you going to do about it?" he asked.

"That depends on a couple of things. You said you saw Taylor in the Raffneyville bar last night. Did you see him when he came to the house, later on?"

"Taylor?" Ben repeated, as if he had difficulty in

identifying the name. "Oh, the cop. No, I didn't even know that he came to the house."

"Now tell me why you were so anxious to examine Vivian's room, and then this morning you forget all about it. Did something happen?"

Ben's hand came out of the drawer, and he was holding a revolver. He pointed it at Hank. "Sure," Ben said. "Plenty happened. You know just about everything."

"Put that down," Hank said steadily.

"What for? I can't be in much worse trouble. Give me one good reason why I shouldn't use this." His lips twisted wryly. "Liz will say it was self-defense, I'm not worried about that."

"I'll say nothing of the kind!" Liz said sharply. "Ben—don't!" She forced a smile as she moved toward him, but her voice was close to breaking. "Ben, are you crazy? We have enough trouble, do what I say, please—"

Ben hit her and knocked her out of the way. As Ben turned with the blow, Hank slapped the gun aside and smashed out. His fist connected with Ben's jaw, and Ben leaned back and his knees buckled. He fell slowly and gracelessly, and Hank grabbed the gun.

Liz, on her knees, crawled over to him. "Ben," she whimpered. "Ben—are you hurt?" She lifted his head, pillowed it and uttered moaning sounds as she caressed his face.

Anger, contempt, gratitude, amazement—Hank wasn't sure what he felt, but he turned abruptly and walked into the next room. It was Liz's, and he sat down on the bed and broke open the gun. While he removed the bullets and pocketed them, he heard Liz step to the bathroom, he heard the sound of running water. He dropped the gun on the bed, stepped over to the bureau and picked up a bottle of perfume. He smelled it and made a face.

He supposed Ben would be in police hands tonight or tomorrow. He'd start by lying and accusing Hank, but he'd break easily. He'd sob and get hysterical and blurt out

139

everything he knew. His story would be distorted and defensive, and it would involve Hank nicely.

He turned around when Liz entered the room. She came in slowly, uncertainly, and her face looked drawn and scared. Her cheek was puffy and the skin was red where Ben had hit her. Her eyes, large and pale, were dulled with worry.

"He—he didn't mean it," she said awkwardly. "He wouldn't have done anything. Not Ben."

"No?" Hank felt himself blaze up with anger. "Liz, can't you admit anything against Ben? What are you defending him for?"

She seemed to shrink away, but her eyes remained fixed on Hank and never moved. "I have to," she said.

"I'm sick of this," Hank said coldly. "You and your beloved brother—you pretend you're friends of mine, while you lie and cheat and act up. I've had enough of it."

Liz shivered. "You think Ben killed her, don't you?" she said.

Hank shook his head. "No. He's too scared, he gums up everything he touches. Vivian's murder was neat, efficient, but Ben couldn't have killed her without a scene. He'd have to get drunk first. Then there'd be a fight or a brawl, because he can't do anything until he's worked up and half out out of his mind."

"What do you mean?"

"Look at the mess in there. Lamp busted, a chair knocked over. Ben can't plan a thing out and then execute it, he's incapable. He even had to send you to get the orchids back. He's never faced a thing in his life. Everything that has to be done for him—you do. And maybe that includes murder, too."

"You believe *I* committed murder?" Liz asked in astonishment.

"I hadn't thought of it. I guess you might have, but I'd have to look at the evidence a little more closely."

"Hank, don't say things like that. Please." She sat down

140

heavily on the bed. "My whole world is falling apart, I don't know what to do. I *have* to help Ben, and I can't. I can't undo what's happened, and it's all wrong. Just everything is wrong. Dick Marlin always helped, I counted on him, and now he says Ben cheated him and has to take his medicine. All Dick is interested in is money. I hate money, I wish I'd never been born."

"If it's a matter of money, how about Ron? Maybe he can lend you some."

Liz shook her head. "I couldn't ask him. It wouldn't be right."

Her answer was so unexpected and so simple in its candor that for an instant Hank wasn't sure he'd heard right. Her words didn't jibe with the Liz he'd seen up to now.

Hank approached the bed. "Liz, do you mean that?"

"Why, of course," she said.

She looked up at Hank. Her face was pale and distorted with weeping, but her long, high throat was lovely as a song bird's. She reached out and took his hand.

"Liz," he said. "What are you after?"

"I wish I knew. I guess I just want something clean and decent to believe in." Her fingers tightened on his wrist. "Before you came here, Ben and I were talking and he told me how he'd cheated and stolen and fixed up the books. At first I was shocked and angry; I started to blame Ben, and then I realized it was really my fault. I'm older than Ben, I brought him up and I got him into this. I introduced him to Dick Marlin and I was proud and pleased that Ben was making so much money and I never asked him any questions. Maybe I could have stopped him. Hank, how could I have been so stupid?"

Hank dropped his other hand on Liz's head and stroked it gently. Her hair was soft and silky, and the warmth of her scalp penetrated to his fingers.

"Why tell me?" he asked.

"Because I'm sick of lying, and I need somebody on my side. Somebody I can trust."

141

"Then tell me what you've been holding out."

"About Ben? You guessed most of it. He did collect the money from Vivian on Saturday, and then keep it. He didn't intend to steal, he was going to give it to Dick Marlin, but—"

"Ben stole three thousand dollars. Don't make excuses, Liz. Just tell me what he did with it."

"Yes," she said quietly. "He lost it, gambling."

"What!" Hank exclaimed. "You mean he's actually that dumb?"

"You don't have to be so superior," Liz said, with spirit.

"Sorry," Hank said. "What did you do when you found out he'd lost the money?"

"I said he had to tell Vivian and see if she'd give him a chance to pay it back. He sent her the orchids Sunday morning, by way of a peace offering, and in the afternoon he went to see her. She was dead, and he got panicky and ran out of the house."

"Maybe," Hank muttered. He was less sure, now, that Ben was innocent of murder.

Liz went on as if she hadn't heard Hank. "I realized that Ben had to get those orchids back, otherwise they'd be traced to him and he might even be accused of the murder, so I persuaded him to go back to the house. I waited outside, in the car, but when he opened the door, you called out and he ran away again. He had the shakes, Hank. They were so bad I had to quiet him down, and later on he couldn't even drive the car. Then, after he seemed a little better, I went to get the orchids."

Hank nodded. "Thanks for telling me," he said. He supposed he ought to be happy, because here was the proof that Vivian had been dead before he'd even gotten there. But he realized Liz's statement, here, under the stress of emotion, was nothing to count on. Besides, Ben would never confess to that first visit, and Liz would probably back him to the hilt.

As if she had read Hank's thoughts, Liz said, "You won't

repeat what I told you, will you, Hank? Because I wouldn't admit it to anyone else. I couldn't go against Ben, could I?"

"Sure," Hank said wearily. "Sure. I know that."

Liz glanced up, but she said nothing. Her face was sad, and for some reason it seemed to Hank that she was sorry for him.

"It kind of sours everything, the way we met," he said. "If it weren't for this mess, we could have had some fun together."

"I don't want fun," she said, in a monotone.

"No? Then what do you want?"

"Love," she said in a whisper. "Don't you?"

"Maybe," he said. "Except that I don't do things by halves, and I hate to get slapped down. So let's admit we're on opposite sides of the fence, and stop pretending."

She made no move, and after a moment or two Hank reached down and lifted her, and she seemed to float up. But she averted her eyes, and her lips were pinched tight. He held her head against his chest and he stroked her gently and she made murmuring sounds. He felt the strength rise up in him and he thought of the time he'd first fallen in love with Sherry, and he wondered precisely when he'd given up saying it could never happen again.

He inflated his lungs and he said in a buoyant voice, "You know what?"

Liz leaned back to look up at him, but she still seemed worried and unhappy. "No," she said. "What?"

Then he heard Ben's heavy, labored breathing, and he turned and saw Ben standing in the room. Liz drew away, there was nothing left of the magic between her and Hank.

Ben stared, a wry smile pulled at the left side of his mouth. He spoke wearily. "Look, I'm a fool. I don't know why I did that before. No sense to it. None at all."

"Oh, Ben!" Liz said. The last trace of worry left her face, and her eyes were warm and tender, her mouth relaxed. There was a soft radiance to her, and a love that forgave everything. She hardly seemed to notice Hank as he strode past her and stalked out.

He had dinner alone, in a good restaurant, and then he went to Mario's and waited.

He was still dazed by what had happened at the Brownes'. Because Ben apologized, Liz forgot he'd just assaulted Hank with a deadly weapon, and with intent to kill. So what was she, anyhow? Loving heart, filled with compassion and with gratitude that the danger was past, or a twisted neurotic, so fixed on her brother that no other man could ever mean anything to her?

Hank wondered what she was doing now. Taking care of Ben, probably. Except that maybe she was thinking of Hank and asking herself how she could have let him go. But, whatever, he was certain that she had to do something, prove in some way that she was free of Ben, before Hank would so much as touch her again.

He shook his head, and his mind swam in circles. Stick to simple things, he told himself. Concentrate on self-preservation, and on Taylor and his grudge. That was the number-one problem. Liz and Ben were a side issue, they were mixed up with Marlin in embezzlement and in crooked, real-estate deals. The police would handle them in good time, and without Hank's help. Whereas Taylor—

Hank picked up his almost empty glass, and set it down with a thud. Taylor had just come into the bar.

He saw Hank and crossed over to the table. On his way, Taylor called out to the bartender. "Couple of beers, Mac." He sat down, a cheerful guy, healthy and uncomplicated.

"Heard the news?" he said. "Mrs. Drury, she admitted she'd gone to see Vixen." Taylor broke into a grin. "Hank, you gave us the wedge."

"She confessed?" Hank asked in surprise.

"Hell, no!" Taylor loosened the top button of his shirt, watched the bartender bring the beers. Taylor picked his up and sniffed. "Smells good, huh?" he said. He took a long

144

swallow and savored it. Then he returned to the subject of Edith Drury.

"No confession," he said. "All she admits is, she went there to see Vixen. Claims she felt too faint to drive in the heat, that's why she took the bus. She says she wanted to see Vixen and ask her to lay off her husband. Threatened a suit for alienation of affections. But Vixen wouldn't let her in the house, so they spoke through that speaker system for a while, and then Mrs. Drury went home."

"The police believe that?" Hank asked.

"What are we going to do? Me, I figure Mrs. Drury would bust down the door, not to speak of putting her hand on the knob and opening it. But she says she was scared as a goddamn virgin." Taylor lowered his voice over the last word, as if it wasn't decent to pronounce outside of church. Then he went on with what he'd been saying. "She says she got to the door and then she lost her nerve, and the whole damn Homicide Squad can't break her down."

"Why tell me?"

Taylor looked surprised. "With her out of the picture, it comes right back to you. You see that, don't you?"

"I heard Marlin was next," said Hank.

"Him?" Taylor snorted. "Decker hasn't got around to him yet, and Marlin'll have his troubles, and so will this guy Browne. But it won't be on account of a homicide. And that's straight from the horse's mouth, so now let's get down to business."

With a thump of his elbow Taylor dismissed the entire mass of evidence that the Homicide Squad was sifting. For him, the facts of life were right here—the table, the glass of beer, and the man sitting opposite him.

"So let's talk about that tan suit of yours," said Taylor. "I took it away from the cleaner, I got it in a safe place."

"You think that cleaner can't do a good job on it?" Hank said coolly. "Maybe you want to recommend someone else."

"The cleaner's okay," Taylor said. "Now how long do

145

you figure it'll take me to match that little piece that got torn off?"

"The trouble is," Hank said, "if you do that, you have to explain how you knew about it."

"I made a lucky guess."

"And then—the graft. One hundred dollars, Taylor, and I can prove it."

"You're off your rocker," Taylor said. His brown eyes under the long, dark lashes stared steadily. "Why did you kill her?" he asked. "For the three-thousand bucks, or on account you wanted a roll in the hay, and she wouldn't?"

Hank frowned. Act sore. Let Taylor build up the idea, let him make something out of it.

"Lay off," Hank said, "or I'll get you kicked out of the department. And I'm not kidding."

"Sure. Pisani told me all about it."

"I don't need Pisani," Hank said. "Believe me, I'm going over his head."

"To the Commissioner?"

"Tomorrow morning," Hank said, "I'm going to the D.A.'s office and tell them you took a bribe, tried to frame me for impersonating an officer, and sought to interfere with my business. And I can back it up, too. Switchboard girl, florist. And Vivian's records show one hundred bucks to Taylor. So don't kid yourself."

"You play dirty, don't you?" said Taylor.

"When I have to."

"Know where this'll land yon?"

Hank nodded. "I'll lose my license, and I expect to be held as a material witness in a homicide case, but I'm going through with it."

Taylor studied his beer. "Funny how you can push a guy too hard, and he blows his top and you both get hurt." Hank made no comment, and Taylor went on. "So maybe I better lay off, drop the impersonation charge and forget about that dough you banked. Looks like I goofed it, huh?"

146

For a moment, the direct effrontery knocked Hank off balance. He had to heat up his anger again. He said slowly, "Your word's about as good as this stain on the table." He lifted his glass, and with his finger he wiped off the small ring of moisture.

"What do you want?" Taylor said. "An affidavit?"

Hank let the remark sink in. "Not a bad idea," he said thoughtfully. He fiddled in his pocket and took out the civil-service forms. Squinting at them, he pointed to the separate character blank. "Sure," he said. "How about it? You can sponsor me, Taylor."

"You kidding?"

"No. Because if you try to smear me after signing this, you'll look kind of sick, won't you?"

"Let's have it," Taylor said. He read the printed statement aloud. "I, the undersigned, know the applicant and testify to his good moral character." He put the form down and studied Hank. "What kind of a job you want? Investigator or something?"

Hank shrugged. "Just sign it," he said. "You know what the deal is."

Unblinking, Taylor unclipped the pen from his breast pocket and scrawled his name, with rank and badge number.

"Date it," Hank ordered.

Taylor looked up at the calendar on the wall. "The fifteenth, huh?" He inserted the date and handed the paper to Hank. "Just one thing," Taylor said. "When I can really nail you, I'm going to do it."

"Taking a big gamble, aren't you?" Hank said sarcastically.

"Call it that." Taylor stood up, shoved his hand in his pocket. "See you tomorrow, huh?"

He stopped at the cash register, and Hank heard Taylor's high, nasal voice. "I'll take the check. Sure, all of it, for me and my friend."

Then he went out, a medium-sized guy with heavy

147

shoulders. Cheerful, untroubled. Win or lose, all the same to him. The perfect temperament for a cop. Or a murderer.

12

Hank wound up his business quietly, without fanfare. A notice to his landlord, effective at the end of the month, and a registered letter to the department of licenses, please note enclosures. Then he called Jean.

She'd made arrangements for leaving the lake and she sounded happy and efficient, pleased with the chance to serve him. Another family was taking the cottage this afternoon, and the Greenleafs were packed and ready to go. No, Hank didn't have to bother calling for them, some friends were driving in, they had a station wagon and plenty of room for baggage. They'd be home early this afternoon.

Hank felt left out of it. His family was supposed to depend on him. And instead, Jean took charge. She acted as if she was married to him.

He felt vaguely despondent and Jean's flat, businesslike voice lingered metallicly in his ears. Momentarily it was overlaid with another voice, and he smiled at the recollection. Then his smile twisted at the corners.

Liz. Swept by the hurricane of external events and her own inner conflicts, she was heading into a crisis—and it was a tough one. With Ben falling apart and Marlin walking out on her, she needed something solid to hang on to.

But so did Hank.

Frowning, feeling like one of those trick, celluloid balls

148

caught in the jet of a fountain and balanced there forever, or until somebody turned off the water, he went down in the elevator. Liz and Jean, the two jets of the fountain. And in the basin below, like spent, motionless water, Celia. Killed because she'd seen too much.

Hank took his car from the parking lot. He decided to stop in at the finance company later on in the afternoon and ask for his old job. They'd told him once that he could have it any time he wanted it. And if he didn't really want it, he sure needed it. He supposed he'd get over his feeling about cars. A car was a car, he was driving this heap and he felt all right; he could live with cars again, unbothered.

He parked across the street from the Kendrick Arms, cut his motor and went into the building. The lobby was broad and swank, the walls were stamped with ceramic medallions, and the carpet underfoot was reassuringly soft. He went up to the seventh floor and rang the bell.

The maid who opened the door was smartly dressed in a starched uniform. Yes, Mr. Drury was home, she said. Would Mr. Greenleaf wait in the living room?

It was a first-class decorator's job, with luxurious drapes, custom-made furniture and an enormous gray, circular couch fitted against the far wall. The portrait over the mantel was probably Edith Drury's father, who'd founded a fortune and whose memory still reigned. Hank was staring at the picture when Ron came in.

He looked haggard, and the limp hand he extended drooped with discouragement. There was sadness and resignation as well as kindliness in his smile.

He brought Hank to a small couch which, with a chair and a round, polished table, formed a cozy unit at the far side of the room.

Hank came to the point at once. "Ron," he said, "I'm quitting. You got my Raffneyville report, and it amounts to nothing. I'm no help, you had a crazy idea to begin with, and I messed it up. So—here." He handed Ron a check for a thousand dollars.

149

Ron waved it away. "What are you talking about?"

"I can't take money for something I haven't done, and can't possibly do."

"Nonsense, Hank. Let's think this over and find a new approach, because I need you." He glanced at the arched entrance to the room, and he lowered his voice. "She walked all over the police department yesterday. I think she enjoyed every minute of it, and now I'm worse off than ever. She's a dynamo."

"Nothing I can do, Ron. I'm sorry, but I'm not even a licensed investigator any more. I have no right to work for hire."

"But, I've paid you already. Hank, try to understand. For a while I had my name in the papers, people looked at me and pointed me out, but now Mrs. Drury is being head-lined and I'm nobody."

"You ought to be glad you're out of it."

"I'm not out of it, because the Marlin enterprises are breaking up and I'm the chief creditor. I hold some big mortgages, and the police suspect Ben of doctoring the books and Marlin is headed for bankruptcy."

"I have nothing to do with that."

"But you will, if I take this check. Because once I fore-close, Marlin goes broke and a receiver will be appointed to handle his affairs, and I'll be dragged into it. My finances will come under the scrutiny of a Federal court, I'll be questioned about my motives and all the surrounding cir-cumstances, and that means—" Ron broke off suddenly and cleared his throat. His eyes darted toward the doorway, and Hank turned and watched Edith Drury sweep into the room.

"Mr. Greenleaf," she said, extending her hand. "I just heard you were here."

Hank stood up and shook hands. The woman who faced him had blossomed forth. Her flowered print dress set off bolder curves, and instead of a blanket-roll of a bosom she presented large, full breasts, topped with a shaped bra.

Her eyes flashed, and her mouth glistened with the purplish hue of the newest lipstick.

This, Hank told himself, was what the challenge of battle did to Edith Drury. Or, perhaps, the cause was the demise of her rival.

"I'm sure you've finished with whatever you were talking about," she said regally. "Ron, I'd like to speak to Mr. Greenleaf, alone. You can go into your study."

Drury's eyes clouded. "Why, yes," he said. "Of course. See you later, Hank." He trotted off obediently.

She sat down on the small couch, and Hank took a chair opposite her. "Well," she said. "The two of you have certainly become friends."

"Why not?" Hank said. He gave her a hard, straight stare, and she returned the look without flinching. "What did you want to talk to me about?" he asked.

"I want you to find me a cook," she said coldly. "Remember Celia?"

Hank tensed up, and he hesitated for a second or two. "Celia?" he said, and he sounded casual enough. "Where do I come in?"

"In one of your reports you said you'd gone to Raffneyville and spoken to her. In a rare burst of confidence you called her a good cook, and Ron agrees wholeheartedly. My cook is leaving at the end of the month, and I imagine Celia is looking for a job."

"Then offer it to her."

"I can't locate her. She doesn't answer the phone at Raffneyville and she told her son—Dick Marlin gave me the name—that she wasn't coming to town on her day off. So where is she?"

"I don't know," Hank said. "And I'm not in the employment business."

"But you're in the business of finding people, she's apparently missing, and I do need a cook."

But not a dead one, Hank thought, and he wondered whether Edith Drury knew. "Try the police," he said gruffly.

"Lieutenant Decker? Hardly."

"Well, I can't help you," Hank said. "Anything else?"

"There certainly is," she said. "I understand that you told the police you'd seen me take a bus in the direction of Miss Vixen's house, last Sunday noon."

"That's right."

"I would have thought that you had a moral responsibility toward a client."

"My moral responsibility," he said, "is to tell the truth."

"How admirable!" she said sarcastically. "Perhaps I should follow your example and tell the police a few truths about you."

"Go ahead."

"I'll tell them how you gave me a totally false picture, and that I sometimes find it hard to believe you were quite as incompetent as you seemed."

"I gave you the facts," he said drily. "You said they were dull. Remember?"

"They were misleading," she remarked, "and the newspapers were able to add quite a few. Such as the details of her love life, the different men she had—when I read that, I realized that Ron wasn't really carrying on an affair at all. You gave me to understand that he was the lover of this mysterious, tragic actress, but according to the papers, he was just one of the crowd." He voice sharpened, and there was a nasty ring to it. "Why did you withhold all that? What were your motives?"

"You hired me to follow him and report, and I obeyed instructions. And the way things shaped up, it's lucky I did." Hank felt the anger creep into his voice. "Otherwise, he might have been accused of murder. And for all I know, he did do it."

Edith Drury smiled. "That," she said, "is an interesting observation. Because if you think he might have, it means he really has no alibi. And neither have you."

Hank realized the blunder he'd made, and he gave her a sharp look. She gazed back with unconcealed triumph.

152

"No one," she said, "can make a fool of me."

"No one," Hank retorted, "is trying."

She grew affable then, as a politician becomes affable after pulling a fast one, "I have no animosity toward you," she said, "but I suggest that you take no part in any of my husband's little escapades."

"I never have," he said, "and I don't expect to."

"Then what were you talking about just now?" she demanded.

Hank stared. He saw a handsome woman who exuded energy and certainty in a steady stream, like water gushing from a tap. She was active in women's clubs and was president of several, and she knew how to handle people and to get what she was after.

But not from Hank Greenleaf. And if she was jealous without any actual foundation, so much the better for Ron. Hank wasn't going to sabotage the little guy.

"Mrs. Drury," he said, "I did a job for you, and it's over. I suggest we drop this whole subject."

"And I suggest," she said, "that you'll regret this rather high handed attitude."

Which, Hank realized, was a suggestion that was quite likely to come true.

He was aware, then, of someone else in the room, and he turned his head and saw Ron Drury standing in the doorway. Ron was smiling broadly, as if he'd been eavesdropping and liked what he'd heard. Now, as Hank noticed him, Ron came forward.

Edith Drury sat up straighter. "Ron," she said, in a perfectly calm voice, "I didn't see you. Mr. Greenleaf was just leaving. We've had such an interesting talk, haven't we?"

Hank nodded stiffly and got up. "You understate it," he said. "And I hope you find your cook." He wheeled and marched out.

In the evening, he saw Taylor again.

13

at six-thirty A.M. on the dot, same as always. He was on his feet maybe three seconds afterward, and slipping into his shorts. He slept in his skin, but Amy liked nightgowns, soft thin ones. He turned and looked at her, sleeping there like a kid. She had a nice small nose, and a body he could almost feel like it was still curled around him. He leaned down, thinking maybe he could kiss her, but she moaned and made movements and he pulled back, on account he didn't want to wake her up.

He moved quietly. He had a hunch that this was going to be his day, and it was a feeling he could almost touch. It was practically down there in his broad, squat feet. After a quick glance at Amy to make sure she wasn't watching, he bent down and touched his toes. He felt sort of foolish. All that happened was, he noticed the toe nails were too long, he shoulda cut them last week. Here they were making holes in his socks and Amy'd bawl him out on account of she had to darn them.

He dressed without making any noise, figuring for once he could outwit the kids and have his coffee alone, without their getting up his backside, like they usually did. He hardly washed, those kids had ears that could hear a guy rub dandruff out of his scalp next door. He slid into his clothes and sneaked into the kitchen so quiet he couldn't even hear himself. The refrigerator hardly clicked when he opened it, and he took out the coffee and left the door the way it was, without closing it, so they wouldn't hear it and know he was up. And so when he turned around, there they were, standing there and watching him.

154

"Daddy," Mamie said. "I'm hungry." And Joey grinned like a lousy little angel and piped up, "Me too."

So Mitch lost out again. He poured their milk, and every time they opened their yaps he said, "Shut up, Mommie's sleeping." They kind of giggled and spilled their milk all over the place, and he stuffed some cereal in them and then took them to the bathroom. And if they weren't exactly clean, the water was dripping off them so Amy'd know they'd gotten washed.

She showed up around the time he was ready to leave, and like always she outwitted them and had them playing with a couple of bottle-tops or something, which left him and Amy alone at the door. She gave him a kiss that would last all day, and he went out like he'd won the Irish sweepstakes.

After that it was pretty much like all the rest of the mornings. Mitch walked to the avenue and waited on the corner and then the bus came along and he climbed in. He stood behind the driver, legs spread to balance himself against the sway of the bus, and he and the driver jawed a little, mostly about the weather. Then they got to Mitch's corner and he said, "Take it easy," and he stepped out and walked to the brick station house.

He wasn't late and he wasn't early, and he went down to the locker room and put on his uniform. After that he went upstairs and the squad lined up and got their instructions from the sergeant, and he had Mitch down for duty with the Homicide Squad, report to Decker.

Mitch was doing errand-boy stuff all day long, but it took him in and out of headquarters and so he saw the gang and they told him what was going on. For instance, they'd gone to work on this Marlin and he cracked up and admitted how he'd been paying off one bunch of investors with the dough he was collecting from another bunch. It ended up he looked clean on the homicide, but there he was bawling like a kid and saying he'd done wrong and spilling out his troubles. He'd thought if he could unload the Raffneyville place on Vixen, then maybe he could pull himself out of his jam. She'd been about ready to sign and the Browne guy had seen her on Saturday to get a down-payment, and instead, he told Marlin she'd changed her mind. The only thing was, she'd told Drury she *had* paid.

That made Ben Browne the Number One boy, only he'd run out on the cops and nobody knew where, not even his sister.

Decker had a session with her and she claimed she and Ben had spent Sunday afternoon at home, working on some accounts, which was a story Decker wasn't buying. He figured Ben had gone to Vixen's.

Then a funny thing happened. It turned out from a question the lieutenant was asking her that this Ben, he was allergic to orange juice, he couldn't drink it without he broke out in a rash. The Browne doctor backed that up, too, he said he'd treated Ben a couple of times for a bad rash, before tracking down the reason for it.

A lot of cops would have said what the hell, somebody else had a glass of orange juice and why worry. But the lieutenant was a stickler for details like that and he had one of his famous hunches. That orange juice, it became the key to the whole case. The way it stacked up, Browne could have killed her but so could this guy that liked orange juice, and so the guy had to be found, regardless.

That was how things stood when they told Mitch to go up to the Drury house and deliver Mrs. Drury those reports of hers. She wanted them back for some reason, and the Homicide Squad had copies so they figured they could oblige. They hadn't counted her out of the case, either. It was just that this business of getting hold of the orange juice guy came first. Once Decker had that, he'd be pretty close to home plate.

Mitch felt good about it, on account of everything was swinging around and practically dropping in his lap. Hank Greenleaf was the orange juice guy, and Mitch had leverage on him and the only question was how to use it. Still,

Mitch didn't waste time worrying, he'd see the guy tonight. And if Mitch used his head, he might pick up something interesting from Mrs. Drury.

The Drurys lived in a pretty classy joint, and a maid answered the bell and said she'd take the papers, Mrs. Drury was expecting them.

Mitch shook his head. "I got to give them to her, personal," he said.

Mrs. Drury must have heard, because she came into the little room off the door and said, "You're from the police department? You brought the papers?"

She was a big woman and still handsome, and she had plenty inside that summer dress of hers. Mitch gave her the eye and said, "You'd better look them over, Mrs. Drury. Make sure they're all there."

"I'm certain they are," she said. And then added, "But the police always check, don't they?"

"We try to be thorough," Mitch said.

She took the papers and went into a big living room that reminded Mitch of a hotel lobby; you could get maybe eight or ten people on the big couch, and then a few more could sit in front of the fireplace and then some more around the little table. He wondered whether the Drurys didn't feel a little lost when they were here alone, just the two of them. But one sure thing was, they didn't sweat, not with this air-conditioner working.

He watched Mrs. Drury glance at the papers, and he thought of what Amy had said. Change of life. It gave Mitch a funny feeling, like Mrs. Drury was going to change right now, in front of him. Maybe like that movie he'd seen of a flower growing, slow motion that had taken maybe a few days and been boiled down to a half minute. Only she was no flower, she looked more like a volcano.

She finished up with the papers and said, "I seem to have them all. Thank you very much."

Mitch didn't move. He still gave her the eye and said, "Mrs. Drury, mind if I ask you something?"

The question kind of surprised her and she seemed to take him in for the first time. He'd been just a cop delivering some stuff, but now he was a guy talking to her. She looked him over like he was applying for the job of her personal valet.

"Yes?" she said in a brand new voice. "About what?"

"About this Greenleaf," he said. He could see her tense up, and he went on and said, "He was working for you, you must have seen him quite a few times. This stuff he sent you—you think it was on the level?"

"What do you mean?"

"I been around a little," Mitch said, fishing and waiting to see what would happen. "I know some of these private investigators. Sometimes they cut corners, they say they been on the job, and maybe they just been sitting in the nearest bar, having themselves a drink."

"I assumed Mr. Greenleaf was honest. Is there any reason why I should believe otherwise?"

"Well, there's this Sunday business," he said. "He got you in this jam, saying he saw you take the bus. You had a pretty rough time of it. Now suppose Greenleaf went to that house, and got there after you did."

"Did he?" she asked, and her eyes shot sparks and she looked like she was heating up inside, but good.

Mitch acted dumb. "I don't like to throw things around unless I know what I'm talking about," he said.

The remark didn't get him very far. She wasn't going to give, but at the same time he had her hooked and she had to find out what Mitch meant. She turned away from him and started for the window, and then she stopped at a small bar that had some glasses on it, along with a few bottles.

"Would you care for a drink?" she asked.

"With you?" Mitch said.

"I might have a little sherry," she remarked.

"Me, too," Mitch said.

They sat down kind of cozy, and Mitch tasted the sherry

158

and figured it was okay. He could see she was thinking hard, and he knew that if you waited long enough without saying anything, people usually came out with stuff they'd rather hold back. They just couldn't stand not talking. So he wasn't surprised when she popped out with, "Frankly, I don't trust Mr. Greenleaf one bit."

"Maybe I shouldn't say this," Mitch observed, feeling he was finally getting on solid ground, "but I got a hunch he's been doing some fancy lying. Only I didn't suppose you want to get him in hot water. It might mean he'd lose his license."

"I'd like nothing better than to get him in hot water," she said, and she ended up with a snap of her teeth, like she was biting into something hard.

"Then maybe we can manage it. You see, I got this idea he and Miss Vixen were seeing each other on the side. So if he ever said anything about her, it could help."

"Unfortunately he never did. But I'm quite willing to believe that he saw Miss Vixen on Sunday." Mrs. Drury grimaced and added sharply, "With rather sensational results."

"The thing is to prove it," Mitch said. He frowned and dug back into his mind. "Mrs. Drury," he said, "ever see a probation manual of his? A paper-bound book, kind of beat up and falling apart?"

"Yes," she said. "I was in his office one afternoon and he went out to get me a glass of water. I noticed the manual and I picked it up. I remember quite clearly, because I had lipstick on my fingers and I smeared it, and I was a little ashamed." She smiled like you do when something isn't really funny. "The silly little details that stay in your mind. The stain was on page fifty-three, near the top, and I tore it slightly." She seemed to come out of a daze and she said forcefully, "Why? Has it any importance?"

"We like to check details," Mitch said, stalling along. "Have you seen him lately?"

She had, and Mitch got the impression that something

159

had happened, only she wouldn't talk about it. Still, here was one dame who'd be glad to step on Greenleaf. So, after Mitch finished the sherry and gave her a few more tries without getting anywhere, he left.

Back at headquarters, he went up to the second floor where Jub had his big laboratory. Mitch was always impressed with the equipment Jub used, the microscopes and microcameras and that spectrograph thing that cost a few thousand bucks and nobody could work it except Jub.

Jub had on that white coat that made him look more like a druggist than a cop. He was working on that robbery case on Harte Street, they had the guy but he wouldn't talk, and Jub had photographed the tool marks on the busted window. When he was finished, Decker would have the evidence and he'd take a half-hour off and show this guy he didn't have a chance. So the guy would confess, he'd take a plea of guilty and end up with one of his regular visits to the state pen, say for a year or two, and do the same thing over again. Routine police work, but it all depended on Jub. Stuff like that, it was why Jub pulled down a salary.

Mitch pushed over one of the stools and he and Jub talked a little, about Gladys and Amy and the heat and stuff like that. Then Mitch said casually, "Still got that manual from the Vixen house?"

"Sure."

"Funny thing to find, wasn't it? I'd like to have a look at it."

Jub pointed with his thumb. "Over there, drawer four, with the rest of the Vixen stuff."

Mitch found it all right, and sure enough, page fifty-three had a slight tear, and a lipstick stain near the top.

He dropped the manual in the drawer and straightened up. Jub had stopped working and was looking at him.

"Mitch, what was the idea?"

Mitch shrugged. "Nothing much. I like to look at stuff, is all."

160

"You're not kidding anybody, Mitch. Bill Decker knows damn well you're working on some angle, and keeping it to yourself. And he's getting steamed up."

"He's good at that. I know."

"Then get wise to yourself. The smart thing is to go see him and tell him what you know. If you think Bill was tough on you for that Nolan business, you're living in a dream world. Short-cut him, and he'll get your hide."

"Yeah," Mitch said. Jub was right, of course. But to go there half-cocked, before he had Greenleaf really nailed— Mitch wasn't that dumb. So he said, "Yeah, I guess so. I'll drop in and see him some time."

"Now," Jub said. "Take it from me, Mitch, it won't wait. He might even be willing to forget what happened, but only if you go along with him one hundred per cent. And right away."

Mitch frowned. Jub had never said anything like that before, never really tried to push him. And Jub was practically inside Bill Decker's mind, no question about it. So Mitch turned his frown into a grin, slapped Jub on the shoulder and said, "Thanks for the advice. I guess I may as well go see him."

He went out of the lab slowly, on account of he knew Jub was right, and yet it wasn't in Mitch to go off half-cocked. Besides, he'd dreamed so many times of walking in there with the case all tied up, and now he was supposed to spill everything, like Decker was papa and Mitch needed help.

But halfway down the stairs, the idea hit Mitch, and he kind of chuckled to himself and saw how he could do it. Because everything he had, except maybe the manual and one or two other things, pointed to Greenleaf's alibi, which was also Drury's. So why not twist it and pretend he was after Drury? That way, Mitch could tell Decker most of what there was, and then when the time came he could pull a fast one and act like he'd made a mistake. He'd just switch back and put the screws on Greenleaf, and that would be that.

161

The brunette sent Mitch into the lieutenant's office and Mitch sat on the stool like he always did, only he felt a little funny. Because here with Decker, Mitch had to admit that this was one guy he looked up to, one guy he wanted to work for. And if there was a chance to get back on the Homicide Squad, that was the thing Mitch wanted most in the world. And not just to get out of a uniform, or even for those five hundred extra fish that went with the rank of inspector. That was important, but Mitch had to admit that Decker stood for something, and part of it had rubbed off on Mitch.

So it hurt him a little, the way he had to angle things. Still, it was Decker's fault that Mitch was up in the Fourteenth, and Mitch wasn't the kind of guy to get soft in the head and fall apart.

"Lieutenant," he said, "I guess you know I been trying to dig up some information, and I don't want to hold out on you. So here it is."

Decker nodded like he'd been expecting this all the time. "Shoot," he said.

"Well, I don't say I know who done it, but I got a pretty good idea, and I figure it's Drury. He was sore about how Vixen was two-timing him with all these other guys, but what put me onto him is that alibi of his. He got Greenleaf to take the afternoon off and fake that report, so the way it sizes up is, Drury had no tail on him."

"Do you know that?"

Mitch leaned forward and spoke in a flat, urgent voice that was down a couple of pegs from usual. "I took a little trip up to Raffneyville the other night, and on the way I stopped at that service station. When I got down to it, the guy was so fussed up on Sunday, he didn't know what time Drury stopped off. He was there all right, but who knows when?"

"And the rest of his alibi?"

"He was at the house and the village, like he says, so I'm working on this end of it. Which is what Greenleaf says."

"Find out anything?"

"Sort of. I just come from the Drury place, and Mrs. Drury—*she* didn't believe Greenleaf's report. I guess she didn't realize it knocked out her husband's alibi, but there it was, right out of her mouth."

"You're guessing," the lieutenant said.

"That's the trouble, Boss." The last word slipped out of Mitch's mouth, but Decker didn't even bat an eye. "My hands are tied," Mitch went on. "I got an idea that Drury paid Greenleaf about three grand for that alibi. But from where I sit, I can't get a court order to check on it. All I could do was trick Greenleaf into sort of giving himself away about banking himself a nice wad."

The lieutenant looked as if he was thinking about two things at once, and one of them was whether Mitch was talking sense, and the other was what Mitch's angle was.

"It could have been the other way around," Decker said. "Greenleaf could be protecting himself, pretending he followed Drury. And the money could have been the three-thousand missing from Vixen's."

Mitch squirmed inside, but the outside of him looked peaceful, almost happy, as if the lieutenant had said exactly what Mitch wanted him to. "Sure," he said. "I'll work on that. I'm going to see Greenleaf tonight, have a friendly beer with him."

"I thought you and Greenleaf didn't get along." Decker said suspiciously.

"We did have kind of a disagreement," Mitch admitted, "but I got to thinking about it and saw I hadn't handled him right. And like you always say, I wanted to show him cops don't take stuff personal, they always keep their minds open."

Decker's eyes came together the way they did when he was thinking real hard. "If you're right on this, you'll be back on Homicide. You know that. But if this is one of your end-runs with the hidden-ball trick, you're going to be through. And brother, I mean through!"

163

"Sure," Mitch said mildly. "I wouldn't kid around."

"I wouldn't advise you to," Decker said. "Now—even if Greenleaf didn't tail him, we know when Drury started out and when he got to Raffneyville, and there wasn't time for him to get to Vixen's, over at the other side of town. How do you get around that?"

"If he paid for an alibi, he must have needed it."

"And Drury's motive? He knew about these other guys, he was friendly with some of them, so why would he suddenly go off the handle and get jealous?"

"It's like this, Lieutenant." Mitch fished around in his mind. "That three thousand—if I could get a court order and show Drury paid it out—and then go into his reasons . . ." Mitch broke off gratefully as the phone rang.

Decker picked it up and said, "Decker, Homicide." He reached out for the yellow pad that advertised some insurance company and he began scrawling all over it. He bit out a bunch of questions like *who* and *when*, and in between the questions his jaw snapped shut like he was an acrobat hanging onto a rope with his teeth.

Mitch could tell something big was up and he figured if he stuck around, the lieutenant would put him to work. So he kind of eased himself off the stool and made it out the door real quiet. He signaled to the brunette to let her think the lieutenant had sent him out, and went over to the window and stood there, where the lieutenant wouldn't see him.

Mitch heard the phone snap down and then Decker's chair squeaked and he barked at the brunette. "Get me Freeman, and then come in here."

Mitch almost had goose pimples, on account of the lieutenant might remember him and put him on a job that could take a couple of hours, maybe. The lieutenant didn't know what time was, and Mitch sweated it out while he heard the lieutenant talking to Jub. "Jub? Raffneyville just called me, they found the body of the cook. Stabbed, lying in Vixen's room. Tuesday night, they think. Marlin and Greenleaf and the Brownes were there. We're going up, now.

Bring your portable stuff, they want us in, but I'm not moving against anybody here until—"

Mitch didn't hear the rest of it. He was out in the corridor while he still had the chance.

He knocked off at four, as usual, and he was kind of worried that something would go wrong. There was this second homicide now, and the investigation might nail Greenleaf, with all Mitch's work gone for nothing, and him out on a limb besides, on account of what he'd told Decker this afternoon. Still, it wouldn't be the first time Mitch had been in a ticklish spot, so why worry? And, particularly, he didn't want Amy to get upset.

They had some kind of jellied fish for dinner, Amy'd gotten the recipe from Gladys. Little Joey stuck his finger in it and then smeared the stuff all over him, and Mamie tried to wash him off, and it ended up with Mitch on the floor trying to show them how a fish swam. They all got to laughing and Mitch saw what a fine pair of kids he and Amy had, and that made things all right.

On the way to meet Greenleaf at the bar, Mitch wondered like he often did why a girl like Amy had ever fallen for him. He'd never found an answer to that one. All he knew was, that while the world was a pretty sour place for a lot of people, the part of it that Amy lived in had the kind of magic he'd believed in ever since he was a kid. And when a guy had that, he couldn't kick. He might be up and down a little, but never went down for keeps.

He got to the bar ahead of Greenleaf, which gave Mitch time to sit down and think. It looked like he almost had Greenleaf where he wanted him. The manual business proved Greenleaf had been at the Vixen house, but it didn't prove when, and that was Mitch's next step. What worried him most was, maybe Greenleaf was in the jug right now, and wouldn't show up. But when Mitch saw Greenleaf come in, he relaxed. Here was his boy; the piece of luck that was going to put Mitch back on top of the heap. In a way, Mitch felt grateful to him.

165

He said hello and Greenleaf sat down, a big guy with black hair and a scowl on his puss. Mitch settled back.

"What I want to talk about tonight is traffic." he said. "Now you been saying you drove out to Raffneyville. On a Sunday like that, with the road pretty crowded and all that heat, there's always something that happens. Cars break down, there's some sort of accident. So what do you remember, for instance, that we can check on?"

"I thought we had an agreement. You promised to quit riding me."

"Then what did you come here for?"

"To find out if you'd keep your word. To tell *you* a couple of things and watch you crawl."

"You're too sensitive," Mitch said. "You take this personal. The thing is, seeing as how I signed that paper saying you got good moral character, I got to prove it. Because Lieutenant Decker's going to want a few details about that trip."

"Decker isn't interested in me."

"He will be." Mitch cocked his head to the side and studied the big guy. "About that report, the one that says you followed Drury out to Raffneyville—what time did you mail it?"

"There's a post mark on it."

"Sure, but it don't say when you stuck the letter in the box."

"Monday morning, early. I came in from the country."

"I guess I can check that with your kid," Mitch said. "Funny how your kid and mine, they go for each other."

Greenleaf set his lips, and Mitch said, kind of fishing around and with nothing in particular in mind, "Because for a while I thought you'd mailed it on Sunday, from your office. But if you done that, they'd have a record you were there." Mitch waited a few seconds, but Greenleaf kept his lip buttoned and Mitch said, "What's Mrs. Drury got against you?"

"Nothing."

166

"She said that probation manual was yours."

"What manual?" Greenleaf asked. But he looked uncomfortable, so Mitch added, "Clown on the cover, lipstick stain on page fifty-three, that's how she can identify it."

Greenleaf gave up then. He said, "Taylor, you can make trouble for me, I'll admit that, but it's nothing compared to what I'm going to do to you. The graft she paid you—I've got a witness to it." Greenleaf stopped, and made like he had something important in mind. "So even if you managed to get that record book with the hundred dollars marked down—or did Celia scare you off?"

"Who's Celia?" Mitch asked, and he was all mixed up now.

"You don't know her name?" From the laugh Greenleaf let out, Mitch figured the guy was off his rocker. He cut the laugh off and stuck out his head and said, "Celia's the cook. The one you killed at Raffneyville. Remember?"

"Me?" said Mitch. "I'm a cop."

"And a dirty, lousy—"

Mitch didn't bother listening to the guy rave, because it hit Mitch that he was as good as back on the Homicide Squad right now. He hadn't tagged Greenleaf with that one, but it was clear now. How could Greenleaf know she was dead, unless he'd killed her?

"Tell me about it," Mitch said. "Tell me some more, Hank, boy. Because the cops are working on that, right now."

Greenleaf got up halfway and dumped forward and grabbed Mitch by the shoulder. Greenleaf was so sore he didn't know what he was doing, and he had a grip like a machine.

Mitch had sense enough not to kid around, so he just stared and said, "Take your goddamn hands off me. And tell me how you know about it."

Greenleaf went white. He let go of Mitch and rocked back, and then he muttered something and spun around and headed for the door.

167

Mitch watched for a couple of seconds and then he jumped up. "Hey, Hank!" he called out. "Your turn to pay!" But the guy kept going.

Mitch shrugged and walked over to the bar. "What do you know about that?" he said. "Me, I'm stuck with the check."

But that was small potatoes, he had other stuff to worry about. First off, there was the way Greenleaf was trying to hang a graft charge on Mitch, and maybe could, when actually Mitch had turned the money down. And then there was the thought of the gang up in Raffneyville with the lieutenant, and how could you tell what they'd turn up? So it was a race who'd nail Greenleaf first.

Still, the worst that could happen was, they'd have Greenleaf for one homicide, and Mitch would have him for the other. Which would put Mitch back on the Homicide Squad, no trouble there. So he felt kind of cocky, and began thinking how he was going to spend that five-hundred.

He took the bus downtown and went to the Seagrave Building. On account of the front door was locked for the night, he had to ring a bell. The watchman who unlocked for him was a big bruiser, and he blocked off the doorway and said, as if he was looking for an argument, "What do you want?"

Mitch took out his badge and identification card. "I'm Taylor, police," he said.

The watchman studied the card and then got out of the way. "Come on in," he said.

Mitch stepped into the marble lobby. It felt cold and dingy, with just a couple of lights going, and Mitch looked around and said, "Kind of lonely, huh? You been a cop?"

"Thirty years, right in this town. Traffic duty, in the Sixth. Name's McGinty."

"Yeah," said Mitch. He always started off making friends with a guy, so he shot the breeze for a little while before he popped his first question.

168

"This guy Greenleaf," he said. "I guess you know him all right. What time was he here on Sunday?"

"Hank? Never laid eyes on him till Monday morning."

"You sure about that?" Mitch asked.

"You can look at the record. Anybody who comes in this building, at night or on Sunday, has to sign in." He pointed to a clipboard hanging from a spike near the elevator.

Mitch stared. "Greenleaf a friend of yours?" he asked.

McGinty's face was impassive. "You know how it is," he said noncommittally.

"Sure," Mitch said. "Now here's the setup. He mailed a letter from here on Sunday, we know that. So if his name isn't on your Sunday sheet, somebody won't like it."

"How do you know he mailed it from here?"

"Postmark."

"Postmark doesn't tell you what box he dropped it in. And my record says he wasn't here, so he wasn't."

"Take it easy, Mac. I want to work something out with you, so you can keep out of trouble."

"I'm not in any trouble."

"The thing is," Mitch said, "the report was typed on his office machine, so we know he was here."

"On Sunday?"

"Look, Mac, I'm trying to do you a favor. Decker and the whole damn Homicide Squad are going all out on this, and you know Decker. You don't want to tangle with him, do you? So I'm giving you the chance to cover up."

"I'd get it in the neck, either way," McGinty said, looking unhappy.

"Hell!" said Mitch. "You can claim he sent you up for the portable, or maybe you stick his name in the record and then cook up some reason why it's in your handwriting. I want to play ball with you, but if you'd rather have Decker crack down on you, that's your funeral."

McGinty's face worked with the effort of thinking. "Greenleaf came in about ten of three," he said slowly, "and he was upstairs about twenty minutes."

169

"Yeah," said Mitch.

He didn't show his excitement, but the timing couldn't have been more perfect. He finally had the goods on Greenleaf, cold.

14

down in direct proportion to the distance he put between himself and Taylor. By the time Hank had walked a couple of blocks, he was able to think with reasonable misery.

He'd botched the works, and his only accomplishment had been to warn Taylor. Hank had thought the graft threat would shut Taylor up, and Taylor had shrugged it off. Then Hank had made the dumbest play of all. He'd mentioned Celia. He might as well have confessed killing her.

He saw that Taylor had outguessed him and outclassed him. Everything Taylor had done was shrewd, and everything Hank had done was blundering and inept. His only remaining chance—a discouragingly slim one—was to find the murderer before it was too late; but he had no leads, no ideas and no confidence in himself.

He reached the small, white, corner building in which he rented the upstairs front, and he mounted the stairs wearily. He hoped Jean had left. She'd arrived this afternoon with Toby and Hank's old man, and she'd gone straight to the kitchen. In practically no time, she had Toby unpacked, the refrigerator stocked, and dinner on the stove. By now, almost nine o'clock, the dishes were undoubtedly washed, and she ought to be home.

She wasn't. She was sitting in the living-room and talking to Hank's father. Her bag was probably in the hall closet, neatly stacked behind the coats. where it wouldn't be in the way.

She gave Hank a look of concern and she seemed to feel out his mood before she spoke. "Sit down, Hank," she said. "You look tired."

Hank flopped down on the couch. His dad said, "That girl who was here this afternoon—wash some of the paint off her, and she'd be pretty nice. Toby liked her, anyhow."

Hank propped himself on one elbow. "What girl?"

Jean answered. "A Miss Browne. She asked for you and she wanted to take Toby for a walk, but I refused, of course. How could I let a stranger go off with him? I was right, wasn't I?"

"Sure," Hank said. "She should have told me she was coming here."

"Because in your work," Jean continued, "you meet all kinds of people, and I can't take chances."

"You said Toby liked her?" Hank asked his father, and the thought was like a shot of adrenalin.

"He'd like anybody who offered him some ice cream," Jean remarked serenely.

"So would I," Hank said, grinning.

His father yawned and said, "You always did go for ice cream, no matter how tired you were. You could do twenty-four hours on the gallon, and end up fresh as ever." He stretched his arms and went through the ritual of looking sleepy. "You young people can stay up, but for an old man like me, it's been a long day." His smile lasted for the time it took to rest on Hank and then Jean. "Guess I'll turn in," he said.

When his father had left, Hank got up and walked to the open window. He stared glumly at the slice of avenue that was visible from where he stood. The geraniums in the flower box that occupied most of the tiny balcony cut off the view of the nearer traffic lane.

"You're worried about something, aren't you?" Jean asked.

Hank spun around irritably. Then he shrugged. He felt like a pinch hitter, two out in the ninth, watching the third strike go by. So tell her, pour it out, let her share it, that's what she wants. Then he'd propose and they'd be joined for life, never alone, never this solitariness. Or else refuse, cut her out, and the breach would be irreparable. Strike three.

With the thought, he felt sorry for her, and he gave her his full attention. Her too-long nose wasn't too long, it was inquisitive and kind of nice. Her skin was brown and smooth, and she shone with the juices of many glands. He could sign up tonight, and it would be all over. He'd have a marriage, and a mother for Toby. If he wasn't in jail.

And Liz?

He crossed the room, picked up a couple of cushions and brought them over to the window. He put one at each end of the sill. This was where he liked to relax and think, with his back against the window frame and his feet on the geranium box.

"Let's sit here," he said. "Outside."

She slipped onto the cushion like a hen settling over her egg box. She leaned back, she seemed to belong. He climbed through the window and sat down, facing her.

"Jean," he said, "I'm in a mess. But I want you to know, first, that I didn't kill anybody. I'm not a murderer."

Her low laugh was amused. "I didn't think you were."

"A lot of people would disagree with you. If I made book on it, I'd give about four to one on my arrest. Any day, any minute."

Her nose tilted up and her nostrils flared. "How can they arrest you? What did you do?"

"Do?" he said, reflectively. "Do? You know how sometimes Toby will step in the mud or in some soft tar, and for the rest of the day he leaves his mark every place he goes? You wonder how one small boy can get around so much and why the stuff doesn't wear off."

"Yes?"

"Well, I stepped in some mud, too. Figuratively. And the

172

trail I left—" Briefly, he told her what he'd done, and the consequences thereof. But he did not mention Liz.

"It's complicated," he said, when he'd finished his account, "but it's pretty clear that Taylor killed both of them."

"But he's Amy Taylor's husband," Jean said, stunned. "I've met him, I know him. And policemen don't commit murder."

"He gave himself away a half a dozen times. How did he know what I did, unless he was watching me at the Vixen house?"

"I wish you'd told me earlier," Jean said. "I could have talked to Amy. And I remember, the day I went shopping, Toby told Mamie about his swim with you. He was so proud."

"Oh." Hank digested the news. It explained how Taylor had caught on to Hank's lie. But the rest of Taylor's facts—shrewd guesswork or guilty knowledge? Which?

"So let me speak to Mitch," Jean said. "Maybe I can help."

"Stay out of it," Hank said in a voice of thunder.

"Yes," she said meekly, and her fingers slid along the sill. "Hank, please hold my hand."

He didn't move. "I just finished explaining—unless a miracle happens, I'm going to be held for homicide."

"I believe in miracles."

Obediently, he took her hand. The sensible thing was to tie himself down to Jean right now, and get it over with. She loved him. She was loyal, faithful, she wasn't burdened with a worthless brother and she presented no complications. So how could Hank go wrong?

Nevertheless, he felt as if he were giving something up. If Liz ever cut loose from Ben, she'd be reborn, the love and eagerness in her would flame up like a torch.

Hank's heart thumped, and then he grunted harshly. He looked at Jean. "Let's go inside," he said dully.

She nodded. "Yes," she said in a low voice, barely above a whisper.

173

He raised his legs and swung them inside the room and stood up. He was helping her to climb inside when the doorbell rang.

"Who the hell is that?" he said. And he strode to the front door and opened it.

Taylor, standing outside, slid his foot across the sill. "Hello, Hank. Let's you and me go down to headquarters."

Hank jerked back. The thing he'd feared ever since that first moment when Taylor had walked into the bar was happening. Taylor had his evidence, he was cracking down.

But Hank, instead of crumpling and accepting the inevitable, reacted with a kind of harsh, angry gladness. The waiting, the cat-and-mouse game was over. This was battle, and Hank's tiredness and sense of defeat dropped off like a wet, soggy coat.

"Headquarters?" he said. "Better spell that out."

"McGinty told me how you went to your office Sunday, and that about wraps it up."

"Is this a pinch?" Hank said.

"Let's do it the easy way," Taylor said. "Nice and quiet, huh?"

"Got a warrant?" Hank demanded. "If not—get out."

Taylor bulled forward, and Hank levered his arm and got set to smash Taylor and slap him out into the corridor. But when Jean spoke, Hank held back.

"Mitch," she said serenely. "Come in, won't you?"

Mitch puffed up, and walked past. "Evening," he said. "Hank and I have some business to attend to, downtown."

"I know," she said. "He just told me. Wouldn't it be better if—"

Hank shouted, "Jean, don't. Let him arrest me, I want him to. Because it's going to be the most beautiful case of false arrest you ever heard of."

She shook her head. "Please, Hank." Her dark eyes pleaded gently, and her voice broke with nervousness. "I think you're both being obstinate. There's no need to be.

It's awful. I—" She began sniffling. "Each of you—you really think the other one could commit murder. It's too fantastic."

Mitch said, "Jean, I know it's tough on you, but this is what I get paid for."

"It isn't, and you're not on the Homicide Squad and you're making a terrible mistake. I'm going to call Amy, maybe she can make you see sense."

"She has nothing to do with with this," Mitch said.

He stepped in front of Jean to block her off, and Hank's eyes glinted. Let Taylor just touch him, make some motion of restraint, and Hank would stretch him out on the floor. Almost prayerfully, Hank waited.

"Look," said Mitch. "You and I know what the score is, and you're a lot better off if you come along voluntarily and leave the rest of it up to the lieutenant. Because I got nothing personal against you, it's the way things break, that's all." And in a gesture that was almost friendly, he reached out to take Hank's arm.

Hank hit him. All of Hank's pent-up anger, resentment and frustration went into the blow. Taylor seemed to freeze, as if he couldn't quite believe that Hank would assault him. Almost, Taylor leaned forward so that Hank's fist would catch him at just the right angle on the jaw.

Taylor was lifted off his feet and he collapsed, neatly and peacefully. Jean gasped, but Hank paid no attention. He bent down and unholstered Taylor's gun and put it on the table. Then, lifting Taylor by the shoulders, he dragged him into the bathroom and dropped him flat. Taylor didn't even move as Hank slammed the door shut and locked it with the key.

When he turned around, Jean was cowering in fright. "This is terrible," she said shakily. "How could you? And what's going to happen now?"

Hank fingered the key and glanced past her. His father, in pajamas and bathrobe, was standing in the open door of his bedroom, but he was too startled to speak.

"I guess I should have let him arrest me," Hank said, "only I'm not built that way."

"But it's all wrong," Jean said. "To a policeman—you just can't!"

"I did," Hank said tersely. "And there's nothing to be scared of."

"But there is. It's wrong, Hank. I don't know what's going to come of it."

Then the phone jangled, sharply. Jean's head lifted up as if she'd heard the ring of retribution. Hank crossed the room and picked up the receiver. "Hello?" he said.

Liz's voice spoke breathlessly. "Hank, I'm at Vivian's and I need you. Come right away, please."

"Sure, but why? What's—"

The phone clicked in the middle of his question, and he put down the receiver. "Business," he said to Jean. "I'll be back later."

She started to question him, but the banging on the bathroom door drowned out her voice. Taylor called out thickly. "Hank, boy, let me out of here. You don't want to pull a boner like this, you want to use your head, don't you?"

"They'll let you out of here in a few minutes," Hank yelled, "so take it easy. Because if you try to bust that door down, you'll have to pay for the repairs."

He started to hand Jean the key, then, not trusting her, he lowered his arm, "I'll leave the key in the mail box," he said. "You can go down for it after I've left." And he rushed out.

Downstairs, Hank got into his rattletrap of a car, switched on the ignition and shot into traffic as fast as the ancient pistons could pound. He felt an urgency in his bones and he cut across the city at a fast clip, on dark, quiet, side-streets. At the corners, he merely blinked his lights and kept going.

He had no idea how Liz had gotten into Vivian's house, or why, and he made no attempt to guess. She sounded as if she were in danger and he almost hoped she was, just a

176

little bit, so that he could get her out of it. But the important thing was that she'd turned to him for help. "I need you," she said. Hank smiled.

But his help would be limited and he didn't have much time. He'd hit a cop and relieved him of his gun, and Taylor would have the entire police department looking for him. And when they found him, he'd be wide open for Celia's murder, and minus his alibi for the Vixen death. And besides, he'd have to explain his elaborate cover-up, which Taylor had apparently unearthed in detail. Armed with those facts, how could any cop help charging Hank with homicide?

So—how long did he have? An hour? Two hours? In which to do what?

He drove grimly, with preoccupation, and he almost missed his turn into Bierce Street. He had to jam on his brakes and take the corner sharply, with a squeak of rubber.

The avenue looked innocent enough. The heavy foliage of the trees seemed to absorb the glare of the street lights. The houses, set back from the sidewalk, were lit up behind curtained windows. No traffic moved.

Ronald Drury's Cadillac was parked in front of the Vixen house, and Hank pulled up behind, jumped out and strode up the gravel path. The front door was unlocked and he swung it open, strode into the corridor and stamped into the living room. There, he halted abruptly.

Ron and Ben were quietly sipping drinks, and sitting in comfortable chairs that were six or eight feet apart. Liz was perched on the couch between them. Her legs were tucked under her skirt and she was clutching something in her hand. Her face was drawn and pale, and her eyes seemed enormous.

At the sight of Hank, her fist unclenched and the tight ball of her handkerchief dropped to the floor. "Oh, Hank!" she exclaimed in relief.

"What goes on here?" he asked in surprise. "What's happening?"

177

M

Ben rocked to his feet, and the liquor in his highball glass slushed around and some of it spilled to the floor. "Come on and join the party," he said. "Let's all get drunk together, huh?" He swayed on his feet and squinted at Hank. "Say—what in hell are you doing here?"

"I called him," Liz said nervously. "While you and Ron went to the kitchen for a drink."

"Him?" said Ben. "What for?"

"Because I want to say something, and I've been afraid to. But with Hank here, I think I can."

"Are you crazy?" said Ben. "Where does *he* come in?"

"Just shut up," Hank said, "and let somebody tell me what this is all about."

Ron held up his hand. "I wish the two of you would stop fighting," he said. "It bothers me. Forgive me if I preach, but you should have compassion, not recrimination, because nobody is so strong that he can stand alone. And certainly not Ben, who came to my office yesterday and told me of his predicament."

"Why come to you?" Hank asked, perplexed.

Ron smiled gently. "People often come to me when they're in trouble. I told Ben that when a shortage in corporate books is made good, the state doesn't usually prosecute. I suggested that he stay here for a day or so, until I'd discussed matters with Liz. You see, I had a key to the house, and it isn't a place where the police are likely to look."

"And I've been trying to show Liz that Marlin's making me the goat," Ben said. "It's all pretty technical and Liz keeps saying she doesn't understand. But it's certainly not like stealing."

"Don't say that," Liz said softly. "Ben, I've been listening to you and I've been thinking so hard, and I want to do the right thing. I've always tried to make things easy for you but don't you realize that some time, eventually, you have to face what you've done and solve your own problems?"

Ben said, "Sure, that's what I'm telling you." But Hank

drew in his breath with the marvel of what she'd said. Liz, he kept thinking. Liz, you're doing it!

Meanwhile she kept talking, in a low, earnest voice. "Ben, I don't think you grasp what I'm saying, but I mean every word. This is why I called Hank, I didn't have the courage, alone. I'm saying you have to admit your mistakes and stand on your own feet, without me. It's your only chance to be free and happy."

"You mean you won't do it?" Ben demanded in a shocked voice.

"I can't," she said quietly.

Ben snorted. "All those fancy words, when Ron promised to fix it up for me if you'd just do him a little favor. Look— you've *got* to change your mind."

She looked up at Hank and she seemed to draw strength from him. "I can't," she repeated to Ben, "because I'm afraid you'll do the same thing over again."

"But Liz—my one chance, and you're letting me down. I've always counted on you And if this is Hank's idea—"

"Leave me out of it," Hank said, interrupting. "She's not letting you down, and this is as tough on her as it is on you, and maybe tougher." Hank swung around to Ron. "What's this little favor you asked Liz to do?"

Ron made a deprecating gesture. "You know my domestic situation, and maybe you remember the advice you gave me once, that I ought to get someone else. So I asked Liz whether she'd be willing to pretend—just pretend, Hank, so that Mrs. Drury thinks she has a rival."

"What!" said Hank in amazement. "You tried to buy Liz? And with Ben as bait? Why, you little—"

The words stuck in Hank's throat, and he turned his back on Ron and looked at Liz. Her eyes were raised as if in supplication, and he felt her as if she were part of him. Gradually, he relaxed and he saw her eyes glisten, and he was on the point af taking her hand and asking her to leave with him. The two of them, together. Then he remembered

179

he had nowhere to go. Like Ben, Hank faced a dead end.

His anger flared, and he clenched his fists. He had an hour, maybe, in which to gaze helplessly at Liz, while Ben whined and worked on her sympathies. Better call the police now, and get it over with.

Ron touched Hank's arm. "Hank, you do me an injustice. Do you really think I'm capable of forcing that kind of a bargain?"

"Sounds like it," Hank said stiffly.

"Then let me correct the mistake. I believe in Ben, I want to give him a chance, and I'll lend him whatever he needs, regardless."

Ben leaped up and his face brightened. "Ron—gosh—I don't know how to thank you!" He heaved a long sigh. "Say, how about having a drink on that? All of us."

Hank glanced at his watch. It would be quite a haul when the police got here. Greenleaf for homicide, Browne for larceny—

"Wait a minute," said Hank. "Ben, I don't think Ron or anyone else can get you off the hook, because those shortages are only part of it. What about the three-thousand you stole from Vivian?"

"I only borrowed it," Ben said. "I expected to pay it back, but I ran into some hard luck."

"The police aren't going to look at it that way. And why you didn't cover yourself on it, I can't figure out."

"What could I have done?" Ben asked anxiously.

"Plenty. The natural thing was to ask Marlin not to mention that three-thousand to the police. It was a business matter between the two of you, you could have kept it quiet. How come you didn't get hold of him and point out that it was to his interest, as well as yours, to shut up about it? He didn't want his affairs investigated, did he?"

"I tried to reach him," Ben said weakly. "I even called him at Raffneyville, around five, but he wasn't there, nobody was. I spoke to Celia and she was all alone, she couldn't help me. Believe me, I wanted to cover up. But by the time I saw Dick, it was too late."

Ron looked surprised and he started to speak, but his mouth dropped open and he uttered a single word. "Edith!" he said.

Hank whirled. Edith Drury was standing in the doorway, and her eyes raked her husband. "Ronald," she said, "I didn't expect to find you in quite such tawdry circumstances. I think you and I had better go, and leave these people to themselves."

That was when Hank took charge. "No," he said. "We're going to iron this out."

"I'm sorry," Edith Drury said, "but I'm not staying."

Her voice was like acid, cold and biting. She'd defied the police and stepped all over her husband, and now it was Hank's turn. If he opposed her, she'd crush him.

Well, let her try. His chin came up and his eyes shot sparks. "Your husband's been harboring a fugitive from justice, and it looks as if you were in on it, too. So you'll stay and explain."

"Mr. Greenleaf, are you threatening me?"

"You bet I am."

Ben let out a roar of laughter and immediately stifled it. He sat down with a thump, and Hank strode past him and began pacing the carpet. "First of all," he said, "what brought you here, Mrs. Drury?"

She crossed the room without so much as a glance at Liz or Ben, and she stood in front of Ron and waited for him to get up and offer her his chair. When he did, she sat down, crossed her legs and made herself comfortable.

"My husband," she said, "made a fool of himself once, and I decided it was not going to happen again. So when he took this girl out to dinner, I followed in order to find out what they were up to. Following someone is not very difficult, any simpleton can do it."

"Thanks," Hank said drily.

"I trailed them here and I was about to go in when you

arrived. I waited a few minutes, and here I am. And now
that I've explained, I can think of no compelling reason
why I should attend your little symposium."

"My symposium," Hank said, "is just beginning, because
something else happened and the police are working on it
right now. On Tuesday night, Celia was murdered."

He concentrated on Ben in order to see his reaction, but
at Edith Drury's moan, Hank spun around and stared at
her.

"Oh!" she said, with a kind of anguish. "There goes my
cook!"

15

AT EDITH DRURY'S
monumentally insensitive remark, Hank burst out laughing.
It was so ridiculous, he couldn't help it. Then, with the
release of tension, his mind seemed to swing back into
balance and attain a more rational perspective. It struck
him that for the last few days he'd been so engrossed in his
duel with Taylor that he'd been blind to everything else.

Taylor, he realized, was a side issue. Taylor was a petty
grafter working an angle, but also, he was an experienced
cop and he had better ways of dealing with Vivian than
killing her. To suspect Taylor was a mistake.

Hank had no theory and no flash of inspiration, but a
surge of confidence swept him up. Except for Marlin, Hank
had the chief suspects in front of him, and he held the initi-
ative. He was conscious of a strange kind of excitement, of
some inner force driving him, and he turned away from
Edith Drury and approached Liz. He spoke quietly, in a
level, earnest voice.

"Liz, when you and Ben and Dick Marlin left

Raffneyville so suddenly the other morning, it was because you knew Celia was dead, wasn't it?"

Liz raised her face. Her lips were parted and her eyes were solemn, and she seemed empty of everything except a transcendent determination to help Hank. "Yes," she said. "Dick is a restless sleeper and he often wanders around the house at night. He found the body and told us about it. We decided to say nothing, and to pretend we had business in the city."

"Thanks," Hank said. "Thanks for setting that straight."

Edith Drury's voice sounded out, clear and smug. "What a charming confession!" she said. "The four of you there, and concealing a murder which took place while Ron and I were in town. In fact, I was at a D.A.R. meeting that night, and it lasted quite late."

"In that case," said Hank, "maybe you'll tell us about the conversation you had with Vivian, on Sunday."

"I already told it," she said, "and to the police. Mr. Greenleaf, you had been so utterly inept that I decided to see Miss Vixen myself. I discovered you had interviewed her, and had done nothing to further my interests. Apparently, however, you had furthered your own."

"You just gossiped about me?" Hank said sarcastically. "That was all?"

"Certainly not. I told her I'd bring her into court and sue her for alienation of affections, unless she broke with Mr. Drury. In view of the inevitable publicity such a trial would entail, she could hardly refuse."

"That was why she was trying to reach me," Ron added. "To see if I could make Mrs. Drury change her mind."

Hank had his doubts that Edith Drury ever changed her mind, about anything. And particularly, at her husband's request. Still, he wondered what Ron could have done about that threat. Marlin had said that Vivian had practically burned up the phone wires, and Hank reflected that it must have been quite a day for the phone company. Marlin calling Vivian, Ben calling Marlin, Vivian trying to reach Ron and Ron trying to get Marlin. All that phoning, and what did it amount to?

What it amounted to didn't come clear, but Hank had the glimmering of an idea, and he was desperate enough to gamble on his guess. He was far from certain, but he was too wrought up to care. And he had so little time left.

He swung around and faced Ben and started firing questions, hoping to see daylight as he went along.

"Ben, you said you phoned Raffneyville Sunday afternoon. You wanted Marlin, but Celia answered. That's what you said a little while ago, isn't it?"

"That's right."

"What were her exact words?"

"How would I remember?" Ben answered sulkily. "She said nobody was there. Something like that."

"Nobody was there? Or nobody had been there, yet? Think, Ben. Which was it?"

Ben thought. "I asked her whether anybody had shown up and she said no, she'd been alone all day."

"That was at five o'clock?"

"Around then. I didn't time myself."

"Yes," Hank said excitedly. "But she told the police that Ron arrived at four-fifteen. He had to be there by four-fifteen, unless he left town much later than anybody thinks. Ben, you see what I'm driving at, don't you? So you have to be sure, absolutely sure."

"But I told you. She said nobody had shown up, she'd been alone all day and she didn't know what to do about dinner—" He broke off, wide-eyed, as the significance of his words struck him.

Hank whirled and shouted at Drury. "You killed her," he bellowed. "It's clear now. You turned around after I stopped tailing you, and you went to Vivian's. She was sore, she took it out on you because your wife had been raising the roof with her."

"*She* wasn't angry at me," Ron said. "We were friends, we understood each other."

Hank hardly listened. He was still unsure whether he was right, but this was suicide or salvation, and he didn't know which. So storm and blast and hammer, and don't let up. Somebody was guilty: Why not Drury?

"She was angry all right," Hank yelled. "And when she got mad, she raged at everybody and everything. She didn't make distinctions. She must have lit into you like a firecracker and blamed you for everything your wife had said."

"Mr. Greenleaf," Edith said in her haughtiest manner. "I must ask you to control yourself and—"

"Shut up!" Hank roared, and returned to Ron. "You!" Hank jabbed a finger at the little man. "You figured you had the perfect chance to commit a murder and then frame me, because I had to alibi you to protect myself. So later on, you asked Celia to say that you got to the Raffneyville house at four-fifteen, and that's what she said. She probably thought she was telling a little white lie to save you some embarrassment."

"Hank, are you out of your mind?"

"No, I'm back in it. And I see now what a sweet spot that put you in. A detective saying he followed you straight from the restaurant to Raffneyville, the cook saying you got there an hour and three-quarters later. That way, it wasn't possible for you to have been anywhere near Vivian. Not time enough."

"That's right, Hank. Come to your senses."

"I'm doing just that. After you killed Vivian, you drove straight to Raffneyville and showed yourself in the village around five. You said you'd come from the house, and they believed you. And some hick cop took down Celia's statement and let it go at that."

Ben jumped up. "Hank, I always said I didn't believe in Ron. I told you—"

Hank shouted him down and kept hammering at Ron. "Any real investigation, by experts from the Homicide Squad or by state troopers trained to interrogate—they would have broken Celia down in nothing flat. So you

185

had to get rid of her before she could change her statement."

"Hank, tell me what you're really driving at."

"The truth," Hank stormed, "and I'm getting it. You had every detail planned out ahead of time. You paid me a thousand dollars to go Raffneyville, because you had to be damn sure I'd be there on Tuesday night. And that button from my jacket—it must have fallen off in your car, and you picked it up and kept it and then dropped it on the floor alongside the body."

"Button?" Ron said, and Hank looked away for fear of seeing an honest bewilderment on Ron's face.

"Button?" Ron said, and Hank looked away for fear of see-Raffneyville, sneaked into the house and got hold of Celia and asked her to come to Vivian's room. Celia would do that, for you. But how could you kill her? She was fine, decent, trusting, she only wanted to help you. How could you kill *her?*"

Ron blinked, and his eyes went to his wife as if to ask her what he ought to do now.

She stood up, and her breasts heaved with the long, deep breath that she took to steady herself. "Mr. Greenleaf," she said, "my husband was at home on Tuesday night, with me."

"You're lying. You said a few minutes ago that you were at a meeting."

"Don't *dare* call me a liar!" she exploded. "And you'll regret every single word, because you'll go to jail for this. I promise it. And let me ask precisely why you think Mr. Drury would kill that woman. What possible motive could he have?"

Hank stiffened. The police had let Drury go because he had neither motive nor opportunity. At most, Hank had shown a possible opportunity. But motive?

Liz rescued him. She answered from the couch, in a low, teasing drawl, as if she'd been waiting for exactly this moment. "Why, Mrs. Drury," Liz said, "your husband was

186

having an affair with Vivian. Haven't you ever heard of a lover killing his mistress?"

"That's ridiculous," said Mrs. Drury, "because Ron wasn't having an affair. Not with that woman, and not with anyone else."

"You mean he was just pretending?" Liz asked, still in that infuriating tone. "The way he wanted to pretend with me? You mean he *couldn't?*"

"Exactly," said Edith Drury, with satisfaction.

But Ron banged his hand on the upholstery of his chair. "It's not true—not true," he shrieked hysterically. "Not true —you're lying—you don't know. Just because—"

He broke off, but his hand kept pounding spasmodically, like a child's fist gone out of control. His lips blubbered and he raised his head and stared at his wife as if he was seeing her for the first time in his life. Perhaps he weighed the two punishments that faced him, that of the law and that of his wife, and he chose the lesser.

"It's your fault," he said. "*You're* responsible."

"Ronald, are you out of your mind?"

"Yes—I mean no," he said in a strained voice. "Edith, you didn't think I was capable of murder, did you? You thought I was a little nobody, and I was, before I met *her.* For a while you respected me, until you threatened her and she told you the truth. That's why I did it, because she said that if she went to court she'd make a laughing stock of me. She went too far, she called me names and I had to make her stop."

Hank sighed, deeply and gratefully. He had the motive, he'd won. "Then I guessed it?" he asked.

Ron nodded in exhaustion. "Everything. I did go to her house, I had forgotten the contract for the sale of the house and I figured you wouldn't be at Vivian's yet. You said something about the office, but I found her so angry that I hardly recognized her. I lost my head, I hardly remember what I did."

"And when did you decide to frame me?"

"On the way to Raffneyville I realized you were the perfect suspect. But Hank, you see why I had to kill Celia, don't you? I was worried to death, I couldn't sleep, I kept thinking she'd guess, she'd tell the truth, she'd tell it to Marlin or Liz or even the police. I was going crazy with worry, it was awful. You understand, don't you?"

Hank looked at him with disgust. In the deep silence that followed, they all heard a car stop in front of the house and footsteps crunch up the path.

"Police," Hank said. "Let me handle them."

Except for the drawn gun, Mitch Taylor entered quite casually. He might have come to pick up a package or make a delivery. He didn't aim the gun or make threatening gestures, but he had it ready, as a precaution.

"Greenleaf," he said. Then he identified the others, and he seemed pleased. "And you, too, Browne. Stand over there."

No one moved. They were all too stunned by the impact of what had happened. Mitch was aware that something unusual was going on, but he apparently ascribed it to his presence with a gun. He repeated his order.

"Over there, against the wall. The both of you."

Hank obeyed. He wanted to be arrested at once, so that a false arrest charge would stick and make Taylor look like a jackass. Ben, in a daze, got up and followed, and Taylor backed off. Still holding his drawn revolver in one hand, he uncradled the phone and put it down on the table while he dialed a number. Then he picked up the phone and spoke.

"Lieutenant?" he said. "Taylor. I'm here at the Vixen house and I got him, but the whole bunch is here, too, so—"

He stopped, and he listened to the lieutenant's voice at the other end of the wire. The lieutenant spoke for a considerable length of time, and Taylor listened and his eyes grew wide with surprise. He held the phone away from his mouth and he let out a long, low whistle. Then he licked his lips and brought the phone back to his ear. When he spoke again, his voice was confident.

188

"Sure," he said. "Like I told you this afternoon. I'll just keep him on ice till you get here. . . . Well, it was maybe a little luck, Lieutenant, but mostly I used logic. Yeah, sure."

He hung up, and he marched straight over to Ron. "Mr. Drury," he said, "you're under arrest, for homicide. For the murders of Celia, and Vivian Vixen."

Drury said, "How—" and cut himself off.

"Simple," Taylor said. "Freeman, he was up in Raffneyville and he found a print of yours on the knife, he had to work it up a little, but he's good at that. And it matched. Then the rest of the boys, they managed to trace your car. Them Cadillacs, people notice 'em. You want to tell us about it?"

Drury shook his head quickly and then lowered it and held his face in both hands. He began sobbing quietly.

Mitch stepped away, and Hank said to him, "How'd you manage to get here?"

"Asked a few questions. Traffic cop at the corner saw you go by, and then I picked up somebody who'd spotted that crate of yours, and it was headed in this direction. So I took a chance and came over. Took me a while, of course."

"Listen," Hank said. "You're not going to get away with—"

Mitch cut him off and motioned him to the side of the room. "Hank, boy," Mitch said in a voice so low that no one else could hear. He kept one eye cocked on Drury. "Hank, boy, let's forget about a few things. Even that sock on the jaw a little while ago—let's skip it."

"So that you can get the credit for this case?" Hank said coldly.

"Take it easy, Hank. We want to straighten this out. First of all, you got to climb out of that little business of a phony report to a client."

"What can you do about that?"

"Well," Taylor said, "suppose I say that you and me, we were working together all the time, you told me what you'd done, but I said keep your trap shut so you'll still be friends

189

with Drury and he'll maybe open up with you. Which worked out, didn't it? And which is why I signed that affidavit, see? It shows I knew you were okay."

Hank didn't answer. If Taylor presented it that way, Hank would be clean and he could take his civil-service exam. And Edith Drury would be in no condition to bother with Hank. She had other worries.

"The thing is," Taylor said, "I had it figured for Drury all the time. Told the lieutenant so, and my lead clinched it, so he's got to put me back on Homicide. Five-hundred bucks extra pay, Hank, just like before. So you and me, we got to stick together."

Taylor gave Hank a reassuring slap on the shoulder, and dismissed the subject. It was settled, and Taylor returned to Drury. "You want to tell us about it, Mr. Drury?" Taylor asked.

Hank didn't see Taylor again until a couple of hours later, after Decker had finished questioning Hank. Taylor was standing in the doorway of the house when Hank stepped out.

"Well, it's over now," Hank said. "But I still don't see how you tricked Decker."

"Trick that guy?" Taylor said. "Me? It's the other way round, because he has this screwy idea that I didn't play ball with him. *You* didn't rat on me, did you?"

"I kept our bargain," Hank said stiffly.

"Then I don't get it," Mitch said. He took out a small, green book and tapped it with two fingers. "This thing. Regulations. I'm back on Homicide all right, I'm an inspector, but Inspector Second-Grade. The lieutenant, he never had a second-grade inspector before, but he pulled the rule book on me, and I'm stuck."

"What's the difference?" Hank asked.

"The difference," Taylor said sorrowfully, "is four-hundred bucks. That's the cut I'm taking from full inspector. So how do you like that, huh?"

"I like it fine," Hank said. "It makes up for a lot."

He laughed, and he was still laughing as he walked down the path and turned to the left and saw his beat-up car. Then he noticed someone sitting in it, waiting, and his laughter simmered down to a quiet, serene bubbling.

"Hell. Liz," he said, and climbed into the car.

Printed in Great Britain
by C. Tinling & Co Ltd, Liverpool, London and Prescot